Marlie was primed for an argument

She wasn't prepared for Greg's demands.

"Miss Richmond," he repeated coldly, "I would advise you for your own good to stay away from Lyle Kearns."

She fought to keep her voice under control. "Mr. Alston, I have absolutely no interest in Lyle Kearns, or in anyone else, at the moment." She took a deep breath. "And, if I did, I hardly see how it could be any concern of yours. If I choose to interest myself in anyone, including Mr. Kearns, I need neither your advice nor permission. Is that perfectly clear?"

Greg's answer was to step forward suddenly, catching her up in his arms.

Her mind fought his insolence, the arrogant supposition that she would welcome his advances, but her body instinctively recognized in him the source of a fulfillment long desired.

"Miss Richmond—" his voice was maddeningly calm "—as far as you are concerned, both my advice and my permission are needed."

Connoisseur's Choice

Dixie McKeone

Harlequin Books

TORONTO • NEW YORK • LONDON
AMSTERDAM • PARIS • SYDNEY • HAMBURG
STOCKHOLM • ATHENS • TOKYO • MILAN

Hardcover edition published in 1984
by Mills & Boon Limited

ISBN 0-373-02642-0

Harlequin Romance first edition September 1984

CHAPTER ONE

'THAT's just what I needed,' Marlie Richmond growled. 'That was really necessary to the fulfilment of life!' She frowned at the green paint that dripped from her fingers. It trailed down the side of the wooden duck decoy and spattered on the butcher paper that covered her work-table.

While the paint dripped from her left hand she held the nearly full can in her right. She hefted it, judging the weight, the amount of damage it would do if she threw it against the wall, and the release of frustration the act would afford.

Not that a little decorating would do the place much harm, she thought. The chaos of wood, sawdust and machinery that made up the production area of her uncle's wood speciality shop was too overwhelming in its confusion to be affected by a little paint on the wall. The rough lumber which comprised the bins, holding the various sizes and lengths of wood, resembled unfinished packing crates. The odd assortment of bandsaws, band and flap sanders, and the huge automatic carving machine took up most of the floor space. Over everything lay a thin blanket of sawdust. Cleaning only seemed to move most of it from one spot to another. No, a little paint would hardly matter.

The temptation remained, but Marlie Ann Richmond had not been taught to throw tantrums. With a sigh she released her grip on the container and thoughtfully pushed it aside. There was too much paint left. The damage would be worse than the surrounding chaos deserved. She would just have to relieve her frustrations by cleaning up what was already spilled.

'Of course, you understand, that's not the way to do it,' she explained to the half-painted and mottled wooden duck on the workbench. 'The idea is to throw first and worry about the consequences later. My problem is, in twenty-six years, I've never caught the knack of tantrums.'

Marlie picked up the carved bird, wiped away the excess stain and put it on the high shelf over her worktable. It would dry over the weekend, and Monday one of the workers would give it a good sanding, clearing away her mistake. But for the present it sat with splotched green spots on its back and one wing, staring at her balefully with its half-finished eye.

'Is it camouflaged for the army, or are you doing ducks in decorator colours?'

Marlie jumped at the voice and nearly knocked over the can of paint again. She whirled to face directly into a beautifully tailored linen jacket. As she tilted her head her gaze travelled up the lapels, continuing past the strong brown neck, the firm jaw and straight mouth. It met a pair of dark grey eyes that showed none of the humour his remark implied. In the pale blue casual suit, he stood out in surrealistic cleanliness against the background of the dirty, dusty factory. He appeared to be about thirty-five.

Marlie was tired after a day of working in the ineffectual air-conditioning and already irritated by spilling the paint. Angered by the fear that had come with being badly startled, she answered back with a sharpness that was so unaccustomed, she surprised herself.

'We're carving attack ducks for the army—they'll be trained to go for the buttons.' Her answer was as ridiculous as his question. 'What do you mean by sneaking back here?'

Obviously he did not care for being accused of furtive movements. His dark grey eyes which had held a carefully controlled irritation, glinted with anger. His jaw tightened, and he crossed his arms, looking down a well-shaped nose. Marlie felt the power of the man and thought she might have stepped back if the worktable had not been directly behind her.

'Nobody sneaks through an unlocked door,' he snapped. 'Your security system is hardly better than your—' He didn't finish his remark, but the direction of his glance, travelling to the decoy on the shelf, said it for him.

Marlie bristled. Who was he to criticise what she was doing? Even if it had been wrong, it was none of his business. She glowered up at him, feeling at a disadvantage.

He had to be all of six foot three inches tall, but yet it wasn't his height, nor the magnificient shoulders that were intimidating. There was an air of unassailable confidence, as if in speaking he created fact with his words. The power and strength that emanated from his presence lent the additional weight, but Marlie was not one to be put in the wrong with impunity.

She felt his gaze as he assessed her. His eyes seemed to see through her clothing, at the same time as taking in her surroundings and her job. There was something so intrinsically male in that look that she quivered under it without realising why. His was the eye of the casual but experienced hunter, automatically sizing up any possible quarry.

She ruefully considered her clothing and the dishevelment after a day at work and knew she must have been rejected in the same automatic way she had been judged. Her mood darkened, but she was not going to let him know he had affected her.

'Forgive me,' she said sweetly. 'I wasn't aware we were expecting an art critic—but you still don't belong back here. This machinery can be dangerous. Our insurance doesn't allow for visitors.'

He turned his head as he looked over the surrounding equipment with a deliberate hauteur. Despite his attitude, Marlie thought she had never seen a more arresting masculine profile.

'You may be right,' he answered. 'I can see it's ready to jump its mountings and reinforce the attack ducks.'

'I wouldn't be surprised—everything's set on automatic,' Marlie retorted. She forgave herself for blatant untruth, justifying it by thinking nothing compelled him to be insulting. Still, she could hardly believe she was behaving with no more maturity than the third graders she taught during the winter months.

She recognised his elegant cleanliness as the spearhead of her resentment. No advocate of dirt or sloppiness, she was acutely aware of her own appearance. In threadbare jeans, torn sneakers, and one of her uncle's discarded shirts, she looked as if someone had dragged her from the rag pile. In addition, she was paint spattered and grimy with the inevitable sawdust of the factory in her hair.

That morning, in a spirit of fun and a desire to beat the heat, she had put her shoulder-length blonde hair up in two pony-tails that bounced on the sides of her head like the ears of a cocker spaniel.

For him to stand there looking as if he had just stepped from the door of his tailor's, observing her in all her dirt was enough to be upsetting, she reasoned.

She reached up to sweep a wayward strand of hair back from her forehead, at the same time taking a swipe at the small beads of perspiration on her nose. She saw green. Jerking her hand away, she realised there had still been paint on the back of her hand, and she had transferred it to her face. A green line bordered the lower periphery of her vision. She crossed her eyes, agonisingly aware of the paint on her nose.

Marlie whirled back to face the worktable, but the rag she had been using for cleaning up the spilled paint was saturated. The others were just as bad because of a clumsy day. Her last resort was the ladies' room, but she could hardly leave the stranger alone in the shop.

Turning back to him, she eyed him with speculation. He was certainly no thief. If he was, she amended the thought, the cut of his clothing showed he didn't bother with small places like her uncle's company.

Her wondering about him came to a halt as indignation took over again. The corners of his mouth were twitching as he enjoyed her discomfort. Mustering her shredded dignity, she looked him square in the eye.

'Do you have a reason for being here, other than to practise your insults?'

'I'm looking for some merchandise,' he replied. 'I think the shipment may have been lost.'

So he was a customer, Marlie thought, and felt better. Considerably better. Perhaps he would be dropping in from time to time. She resolved right then to start paying more attention to her appearance when she came to the factory. She forced back her shame and embarrassment at being caught in such a mess, and tried to be more co-operative.

'If you go into the office, my uncle will be back shortly. He just went—' Marlie wasn't allowed to finish what she intended to say.

'Oh, no,' he said with authority, reaching over to catch her by the arm. 'I had trouble enough finding you. I'm not sneaking around any more. I didn't undertake a career in locating your personnel. I've got you, and you can find what I want.'

'But I don't know anything about the shipping,' Marlie insisted as he propelled her towards the front of the building. As he kept her close at his side, she was once again impressed by his height. She felt his strength, and her senses were affected by his arrogant masculinity. His aftershave was a light, elusive scent that hinted of sunlit meadows.

Both his tone and his grip on her arm said he would brook no alteration of his decision. The humorous look in his eyes as she tried ineffectually to rid herself of the stain on her nose showed he was enjoying her embarrassment. That was enough to bring out her innate stubbornness.

Let's just see how much satisfaction you get out of it, Marlie thought, and stopped struggling. Instead she walked at his side, determined not to let him intimidate her again. After all, she had been working, and what was wrong with looking as if she had been involved in honest labour?

Her dignity lasted until she entered the office. It was torn to shreds again as she saw the man had not arrived alone.

Sitting in her uncle's desk chair, looking like a princess out of a modern fairy-tale, was one of the most beautiful women Marlie had ever seen. The elegance of the white linen sundress was reinforced by the delicacy of the high-heeled sandals. Her haircut just had to be a creation of one of the leading stylists. Everything shouted she was most definitely from the same world as the irritating male who still gripped Marlie's arm. Marlie did not care for the heavy, musky perfume the woman wore—it filled the office, hanging in the air like an oppressive atmosphere before a storm.

But she of the white linen and platinum-blonde hair looked as out of place in the office as the man. In the litter of a dozen model ducks, sample pieces of wood, and the clutter that a man like her uncle considered necessary for a comfortable existence, she was obviously both disdainful and uncomfortable. Marlie watched with a small satisfaction, because when Miss White-and-bright started to lean forward, she almost put her hand on the desk that was lightly powdered with fine sawdust. She hesitated, wriggled her fingers in fastidious distaste, and put her hand back on her knee. He expression showed the poise of a select girls-school training. By a slightly raised eyebrow she gave her opinion of Marlie's general appearance before she turned her attention to the man.

'I wondered what had happened to you, darling,' she drawled. Marlie could hear the possessiveness in her voice.

Don't worry, dearie, Marlie thought. You can have him for all I care. Still, thinking of the handsome man at her side with a woman Marlie knew must be unpleasant, made her slightly resentful on his behalf. As if it were his fault that she had been drawn to his defence, she made a point of tugging her arm from his grasp. She walked over to the filing cabinets, eyeing them critically. She wondered how much she could remember of her uncle's erratic system. The sooner she answered his question and sent him on his way, the easier her life would be, she reasoned.

'We file by single order and regular customers. Which are you?' she threw the question over her shoulder.

When his answer was not immediately forthcoming she turned, intending to look him straight in the eye. The afternoon sun was slanting in through the half-drawn blinds, and a ray struck her in the face. The green stain that covered the tip of her nose seemed to glow, drawing her focus inward. When she was able to concentrate on him again, the twitch of his lips had become a grin.

'Well, which is it?' Marlie demanded, feeling every inch the fool.

'You might say I'm a regular customer,' he replied with a curious nonchalance. The female, sitting at the desk, gave a low laugh.

'Name of the firm?'

'Alston.'

Marlie swallowed hard. That was the name of her uncle's largest customer, which accounted for almost a third of their business. While she was reaching for the top drawer, the street door opened. Marlie's uncle, the owner of the small factory, strolled in. Howard Richmond opened his mouth as if to speak and then closed it. He viewed the scene with steady blue eyes much like Marlie's, but his were set in a wizened, wrinkled face.

'Uncle Howard, this—' suddenly Marlie realised the stranger had not given her his name, '—gentleman is from Alston's, checking on a lost shipment.' Marlie had no intention of casting a slur on the tall man when she hesitated before saying 'gentleman', but his mouth tightened. Only after she spoke did she guess he would take her pause to be some socially-affected insult.

I bet I know where you learned to watch for that type of slur, Marlie was directing her mental comments towards the tall stranger, but she was thinking of Miss White-and-bright who was clearly bored, disgusted at her surroundings, and distastefully wiping a speck of dust off her white patent-leather bag.

Marlie had known her uncle too long to think he had been fooled by the atmosphere. With an unerring ability to reconstruct what had happened before he arrived, he knew the attitudes of the three in the office. He nodded to Marlie's opponent and turned his attention to the woman in his chair.

'It's too nice an afternoon to be cooped up in this dirty office,' Howard Richmond smiled at her, showing his appreciation of his visitor without being offensive. 'We're civilised enough to have a Coke machine if you'd like a soda—I'm afraid that's the best I can do.'

Well, so much for manners, Marlie thought, blushing. Where had hers been? she wondered. She had condemned Miss White-and-bright for her disapproving look, but it had been Marlie's place, as an employee of the company, if nothing else, to extend some greeting, something more than the brief curt nod she made when entering the room. If her third graders had behaved as rudely, they would have heard from her. She was thoroughly ashamed of herself. Her only excuse was her irritation at the tall man who stood by her side, looking as chastened as she felt. They had been so busy with their battle nothing else seemed to matter.

'No thank you, we'll have to be going.' Miss White-and-bright's attitude to Marlie's uncle was tightly friendly, but the sharp look she threw her escort showed she wasn't mollified.

Then he turned to Marlie's companion, his hand outstretched. 'I'm Howard Richmond. I take it you're Tom Jordon. We've spoken on the phone many times.'

'No, Alston. Jordon, my buyer, is still in New York. This is Miss Joan Owens-Lane.'

Marlie felt herself blanche. She had been battling with Gregory Alston, the millionaire-owner of a chain of exclusive haberdasheries. Her sharp tongue could bring about disaster for her uncle's business and his employees as well. All her wisecracks came echoing back. She had been hot and tired, true, but that was no excuse. It wasn't like her to behave so badly. Was he to blame? No, she decided. She would keep the responsibility for her actions on her own shoulders.

And Mr Fred Owens-Lane was a well-known hotelier, and Marlie was sure Joan was his daughter. She was impressed.

Even Howard, a man not usually caught at a loss, was unsettled that Alston in the flesh was checking on a shipment.

'Well, uh, glad to meet you, Mr Alston. Your shipment is late?' Howard frowned, looking thoughtful. His eyes seemed to turn inwards as if he kept all the company records in his head. 'I can't understand it. We've shipped your last orders.'

Now that her uncle had arrived and taken charge, Marlie sidled towards the door that led back into the factory. She stopped abruptly when Greg Alston, a flick of his glance showing he had interpreted her plan, stepped between her and the door. All Marlie's shame at insulting him, as well as her intention to behave like an adult, were lost under her seething anger. The flicker of amusement in his eye and his hand, negligently braced against the doorframe, added up to a deliberate refusal to let her pass. His eyes looked past her to Howard, but the resolution with which he ignored her showed he was as much aware of her as she was of him. He was having trouble keeping control of the right corner of his mouth. Every time it quirked to smile, Marlie sizzled.

Howard went to the files, pulled out a drawer and extracted a folder with the ease of complete familiarity. He spent a minute examining the top sheets and looked up, chewing his lip thoughtfully.

'I don't have an explanation. I gave Jordon a shipping date of the thirtieth of last month. We had a chance to get a little ahead so we shipped on the twenty-fourth. Everything certainly should have arrived by this time.'

Greg's brows drew together. 'No chance it was over-looked—that it's still here?'

Marlie watched the wide smile transform her uncle's face. He had overcome his surprise at finding the famous haberdashery chain-store owner in his factory.

'Look around you, Mr Alston. We're a small operation. When we pack an order for you, it clogs the entire building. We're climbing over it for days. Sorry it was side-tracked, though. I guess you've got enough to do without chasing down lost shipments.' Howard sounded genuinely sorry, but there was no fawning in his voice. He was one businessman talking to another on equal terms. He did look a little puzzled, however. Marlie thought he was probably wondering, as she was, why a man of Greg Alston's position was chasing his own orders.

'I'll get a tracer on it first thing Monday,' Howard said, looking up. The other three in the room glanced up also.

Their gaze followed his to the clock on the wall. It was well after five.

The time brought out an objection from Miss Owens-Lane. 'Really, darling, we are due at the Smithsons' right now. Can you finish this discussion so that we can go?'

'Sorry, Joan,' Greg Alston's reply was perfunctory. 'Why don't you go on without me? I want to talk to Mr Richmond. You'd be bored. I'll join you at the party later.'

But Joan had objections. She stood, and Marlie gave a mental sigh of envy at the socialite's tall, willowy figure. She thought, though, the blonde was far less attractive as her face sharpened in lines of anger. Her mouth took on an obstinate line that indicated to Marlie a high degree of selfishness.

Don't let her boss you around, Marlie silently rooted for the tall stranger, and then she brought herself up short. After all, it was none of her business, and she should be glad to see that autocratic nature given a setback. Still, she did not feel the socialite was the one to do it, but she was giving it a try.

'I do think, if I could spend my afternoon sitting here, you could return with me for the party,' complained Joan. She seemed to think nothing of the insult she was giving Marlie and Howard. Their type of business did not cater to walk-in customers, so no provision was made for the comfort of clients, but to suggest that the bare twenty minutes she had been waiting seemed like an entire afternoon was a little exaggerated.

Marlie and Howard exchanged glances. Whether or not her statement was true did not seem to bother Joan. She had given an order, and she expected it to be obeyed.

'I'll join you later,' Greg answered, apparently undisturbed. He took a thin leather key-case from his jacket pocket. 'You take my car back and I'll call a taxi or something.'

With his hand on her arm he ushered his companion to the door. Marlie, seeing the thunder cloud had not receded from Joan's face, took the opportunity to escape the room. If a storm broke, she wanted to find safe shelter. She headed for the ladies' room. Finally she could remove the paint from her nose, and she could thank Miss Joan Owens-Lane for the diversion.

The rumble of voices reached her through the door as she washed her face. The cool water raised her spirits and calmed her irritation. In its place came wonder. Greg Alston! The photographs in the newspapers had never done him justice.

Marlie had begun reading the society columns three years before when her parents, because of her father's study of foreign affairs, had started travelling for the State Department. She often read about people they mentioned in their letters, making her feel closer to her parents. In the circles of the rich, the powerful and the beautiful, Greg Alston figured prominently.

No wonder she had felt the power of his personality, the magnetic pull of his masculinity. Few women could remain unaffected by the gaze of those deep grey eyes. Hey, watch it! she warned herself. She knew that getting interested in him was asking for trouble.

Deliberately she forced her mind to the evening and the things she needed to accomplish. She had used a deplorable lack of foresight in not wearing more presentable clothing, covered with a smock. That morning she had been late in getting her clothing together for their two days out of town, and in the process she had forgotten she would not be driving straight to her apartment for a refreshing shower and a change of clothing. Normally she and Howard went out to the cabin at the weekends. On the way they usually stopped at the bank, a store or two, depending on what they needed, and always at the grocery store to pick up fresh fruits, vegetables and meats. For the nth time that afternoon, she looked down at her shoddy outfit and shook her head ruefully.

Just as she stepped out of the ladies' room, she heard her uncle call her name. Reluctantly she went back into the office where she saw Greg and Howard inspecting a carved decoy. It had been painted in surrealistic colours, someone's attempt at creating an ultra-modern style. For years it had been sitting on the shelf above the painter's bench. To Marlie it was jarring to her concentration. She had carried it to her uncle's office, hoping he would either have it sanded clean of the silver-and-black paint, or get rid of it.

'Who did this?' Howard asked as she walked up. 'I don't remember seeing it.'

Marlie had spent many of her adolescent summers running in and out of the factory. While only an emergency could get her into the office, she was as familiar with the workings and history of the firm as her uncle. In the matter of the signatures on the bottom of the decoys, a pattern of dots placed there by the painter, she often outdid her uncle in memory. She took the wooden carving with the offending paint and turned it over.

'What was his name?' she mused over the pattern of black dots that formed a flourishing number two. 'I can't remember his name, but it was that lanky college student who was here one summer.'

Greg Alston quirked his eyebrow in surprise.

'I thought you were the duck painter,' he said. 'Are you sure you didn't make some experiments? I thought it looked like your work.'

As her anger rose, Marlie wondered why this man had the power to throw her so off balance.

'I would never do that to a perfectly respectable duck!' she retorted and turned to Howard. 'The thing has been glaring at me, and I brought it in here. For heaven's sake—and mine—do something about it.'

'Relatives,' Howard sighed. 'Don't know why I hire them. She's been here two weeks and she's driving me crazy.'

'They'll get you every time,' Greg said solemnly. 'I try to stay away from mine, and never accept the responsibility for the ones I can't control.'

Marlie gave her uncle a dark look. His complaint was their private joke. This wasn't the first summer that he had been pressed for help. She had taken the job to assist him, but she couldn't complain that duty alone drove her to it. The factory was hot and dusty, and she had a choice of dressing like a raggedy-Ann or ruining good clothes. But after months of teaching, the work at the factory was a vacation in itself. Still, Howard didn't have to make Greg think she was there on her uncle's sufferance, as if she could do nothing on her own.

But Howard Richmond's mind had travelled elsewhere. He looked up at Greg with a shrewd expression.

'We're wasting your time, I guess. You didn't come here to look at duck models, and a man who probably doesn't know how many stores he owns, seldom traces his own shipments. You said you had something else in mind?'

Greg nodded. 'I did—I do.'

Both Howard and Marlie watched him as he frowned, thoughtfully rubbing his chin with his left hand. Marlie, the more impatient of the two, broke the silence.

'What was it?'

A smile, half sheepish, crossed his face, taking Marlie's breath away. In it she saw the little boy that hid inside the man with the rich and powerful reputation. She saw why his name was constantly in the society columns, most often linked with this or that socialite. His was a smile to melt a stone heart, and Marlie's lacked even a shell.

Careful, she told herself. Don't allow yourself to be drawn. There are too many females trying to snare him now. He's never going to look at a teacher who covers herself with paint in the summer.

The smile that grabbed at Marlie's heart was soon gone. In its place the businessman had returned. Though his voice held a thoughtful hesitancy, he was back to his original purpose.

'I don't know how to explain what I'm looking for. I was in Europe a few weeks ago, and there's a half-formed idea in my head—maybe I should say the glimmering of an idea. What I should like to do is see your machinery in action.' The smile came back for a moment and Marlie felt her heart grabbed again. 'If I'm wrong on my theories, I don't want to look like a fool, so I'd rather not say what I have in mind—until I know it's practical.'

Howard nodded. There was a full understanding in his smile.

'You deliberately came late, hoping you could run the machines yourself.'

The barely perceptible nod from Greg Alston showed he wasn't surprised at being caught with his intentions down. Without a word he peeled off the tailored linen jacket and started rolling up his sleeves. To Marlie, it seemed that an unspoken conversation was travelling between the two men. Greg had not asked for permission to run the machines nor had her uncle granted it, yet they started together for the back of the factory. Both curiosity and a desire to see Greg Alston out of his role as a corporate businessman drew Marlie along in their wake.

CHAPTER TWO

WHILE Howard Richmond gave Greg Alston a grand tour of the factory, Marlie sat on a stool and watched. The men walked from bin to bin, looking at the rough, sawed lengths of wood that filled the large topless packing crates. They were as absorbed as if they were viewing some marvel of science or nature. A running conversation continued as Marlie's uncle answered Greg Alston's questions and listened to his comments.

In keeping with her earlier irritation with Greg Alston, Marlie tried to hold it against him that he was keeping her uncle after hours in the hot factory. They had planned on going to the cabin for the weekend. Since she and her uncle were both riding in the same car, Greg Alston was tying up her evening, too. She held the thought as long as she could, but not being by nature a person who dwells on the unpleasant, her mind kept swerving over to curiosity. Why would a man as rich and powerful as Greg Alston risk dirtying his expensive, tailored suit and his perfectly white canvas shoes—canvas shoes? Who wore canvas shoes with a suit? Marlie let the questions about his footwear go. That was less of an enigma than his poking around in a dirty factory. After all, he had employees by the bushel to run his errands.

Like Howard, she, too, was wondering why he had made the trip to the factory. Maybe he really did want to run the equipment. He certainly didn't come to check on a shipment. Howard had been dealing with the Alston

chain for years, but had never met the big man personally.

The men made an absorbing tour of bandsaws, belt and
flapper sanders and had what seemed to be an inspired
conversation over several electric hand-tools. Then they
threaded their way between the equipment and wood bins
towards the true heart of the factory. Backed against the
rear wall, as if to defend itself from the world, stood the old
automatic carving machine. In its day it had been the
'state of the art'. Modern advances had made smaller,
more efficient models. They were computerised and out-
rageously expensive but, to Howard and Marlie, not one
could compare with the old Howler, as they called it.

Marlie hooked her heels over the top rungs of the stool
and smiled as she considered what Joan Owens-Lane
would have thought about it. The belle of society would
have seen it as an awkward conglomerate of frames,
cables, motor and control box, all painted an eye-jarring
bright orange. For years Marlie had considered it almost
one of the family. When she returned at the first showing
of summer, it was the first thing she visited after saying
hello to Howard.

'Marlie!' Howard Richmond's voice was a combination
of mild frustration and helpless plea. He stood at the
control panel, looking over his shoulder at her.

'What is it?' she asked, wondering if the machine had
broken down. She hopped off the stool, concerned as if
something had happened to a dear friend.

Howard looked sheepish. 'You know, I haven't run this
thing in five years. I'm not sure I remember how. You
show Greg how it operates.'

Why you old liar, Marlie thought. You could take that
machine apart and put it together wearing a blindfold.

She could see his intention and was irritated by his efforts. He was deliberately pushing her and Greg together. Did he think he was playing Cupid, or did he just enjoy the fight? He was perfectly capable of either, she knew. She longed to tell him what she thought of his ploy, but it would be too embarrassing in front of Greg. She would have to settle for raking him over on another subject.

'If I were you, I wouldn't admit that in front of Mr Alston,' she said. 'That tells him we're vulnerable. After all, I'm only here during the summer. If Fred got sick during the winter, there'd be no one to get out the Alston orders, would there?'

'Well, I did know,' Howard spoke up in his own defence. 'I could figure it out or read the instructions again if you weren't handy.' Howard gave Marlie a sharp glance, letting her know she had hit her target.

Marlie's reasons for not wanting to operate the machine were purely vain. Some years before, she had helped Howard during the summer by operating the Howler when Howard needed assistance. Then, three years ago, Fred had been hired. He had proved so steady and dependable that Marlie had not been needed again. She hoped she remembered. If she made a mistake, Greg would be watching. The splattered duck, sitting on the shelf over her workbench, had given him cause to look down his nose at her. There would be no repetition of that if she could help it.

As she reached for the switch, Greg intercepted her. His long muscular arm stretched over her shoulder, turning on the power. Slightly startled, she glanced up at him. His mouth was still set in a straight line, but there were asterisks of laughter at the corners of his eyes.

'I can do that much already,' he said, as if he thought he deserved a medal for it.

'Then perhaps you can handle the rest,' Marlie retorted, a smile taking the sting from her answer. 'Next you insert the pattern. If you'd like to do that, I don't mind. They have a tendency to become weighty problems.'

Marlie pointed to the nearest pattern in the rack of unlikely shapes. She watched as Greg tried to keep his features from twisting into a frown.

Regardless of the size of the item carved, the patterns all measured close to a metre in length. The one she pointed out to Greg in no way resembled the shape of a duck. From the square fittings on each end, it tapered to what appeared to be a long fat steel rod with a curious, off-centred lump in the middle.

The wood, after being carved by the machine to resemble the pattern, had to have the supporting ends cut away before giving evidence of a mallard duck. Even then it was just the body. The head was carved separately and attached with wooden dowels.

Greg eyed the pattern, gave Marlie a doubting look and carried it over to the machine that hummed its readiness.

She watched him as he held the heavy mould, turning it to consider the shape of the ends and the corresponding fittings on the machine.

Marlie felt a thrill of interest as she watched him. The weight of the steel pattern was considerable, making the muscles of his arms bulge with the strain of lifting it. The swelling of the muscles in his forearms and wrists she could see, so it wasn't difficult to imagine what was taking place beneath the silk shirt as it was pulled tight against his shoulders and back. When he knelt, his well-formed thighs strained against his linen trousers.

He's quite a man, she admitted, and stopped that train of thought immediately. Just admire the view, but don't get too interested, she warned herself.

Marlie saw his recognition of where to place the mould in the slight movement of his shoulders and a small indrawn breath. He was silently congratulating himself on his ability to figure it out without recourse to her advice.

His face had been turned away from her as he puzzled over the mechanics, but as he turned his head, his expression surprised Marlie. He was boyishly happy, learning something new, and she could see a hint of pride that, far from being autocratic, was a childish pleasure in showing her he could figure it out for himself.

He's trying to impress me, Marlie was slightly stunned, but there was no denying that look. She saw it every year as her students competed with each other. But to see it on the face of the great Greg Alston was incomprehensible. She denied what her eyes saw.

So you think you're so smart, she thought, but inside she knew she had been rooting for him. Nor did he turn cocky after his first success. Realising the pattern had to be fastened in place, he considered, and chose the correct handle to activate the clamp. He looked to her for direction before moving it.

Well, you're certainly nobody's dummy, Marlie thought. The Howler was designed to be simple to run. Still, as a corporate owner, the management of unwieldy carving machines hardly fell within the field of his everyday experience.

Fair, was fair, she decided, and went to the bin to get him a wooden blank, originally a length of eight by eight-inch timber. It had been trimmed on the bandsaw to make the shaping on the Howler a quicker operation. Silently she handed it to him and watched as he worked out the problem of how to insert it. He checked with her to make sure he was correctly securing the wood in place. Only when he was ready to put the machine in operation did she stop him.

'Here,' she handed him a pair of goggles. 'Put these on if you intend to see anything tonight.'

Marlie enjoyed the consternation. He was blaming himself for not thinking about the sawdust the machine would put out.

One up for the duck, she thought, and by his sharp look, her small win had shown on her face.

He pushed the button and the Howler roared into action. It clanked and growled, throwing sawdust into the air as if announcing. 'Hey, look at me! You talk about a worker, now see one in action!'

'You ham!' Marlie remarked to the machine as it shaped the body of a wooden duck. She was rewarded for her criticism with a mouth full of sawdust.

Greg, who had obviously been watching her, laughed at her for her error in judgment and found himself in the position of trying to get the flying particles of wood out of his own mouth.

So no one won that round, Marlie thought, heading for the water fountain. There was nothing left to do but to wash the sawdust out of her mouth in the restroom, though she had heard there was nothing harmful in swallowing it.

Howard had backed away from the Howler, but he was watching the operation as well as the continuing battle between Marlie and Greg. As she passed him, she noticed the curious, pleased expression he wore.

'What do you think you're doing, leaving me to show him how to handle that machine?' she asked as she went by. 'I warn you, that fellow and I just may come to blows,' she muttered, first making sure Greg was out of her hearing.

'Haven't had a good fight around here in years,' was Howard's comment. 'Besides, I bet nobody ever argues with him. He probably enjoys it.'

Marlie went into the ladies' room, taking time to rid her hair of sawdust while she was there. It occurred to her that her sudden flurry of hair combing made little sense, especially if she were going back out to the machine, but she let it pass without careful examination of her motives.

During the next hour and a half, Marlie sat on her stool, watching as the famous Greg Alston, corporate executive and society playboy, laboured over the making of ducks. Since the heads were carved separately and attached with dowels, he was not satisfied with just running the machine, but with Howard's and Marlie's help, he trimmed, sanded, drilled and doweled those he had carved out on the Howler. Some purpose of his own driving him, he went back to the big machine again and carved out several more bodies.

Marlie had drawn back, letting her uncle aid him with the smaller machines, but after one attempt at each piece of equipment, he continued without assistance.

Howard had located a second stool and joined Marlie as they sat watching Greg work. When he returned to the Howler and put another blank in the machine, Howard shook his head.

'I'd sure like to hire someone with his energy,' he said.

'I wonder what he's up to?' Marlie wriggled on her stool as a sudden, unpleasant thought occurred. 'He couldn't be planning on opening his own factory—'

Howard Richmond gave her a hard look.

'That wouldn't make sense. Too time-consuming for what he'd get out of it. No, I think it's like he said—he's got an idea and he wants to pull it off.'

'Working that hard on something he doesn't have to do?' Marlie countered.

'Mmm, maybe you're right. People don't do what they don't have to,' Howard replied in a lazy drawl. His exaggerated seriousness warned her he was aiming a thrust of wit in her direction. 'I would know better than to—say—try to get a schoolteacher to work during her vacation.'

'You should, unless that schoolteacher planned on inheriting the family conglomerate,' Marlie retorted.

Greg Alston turned off the Howler and strode over to where Marlie and Howard were sitting. He appeared to be a different man from the vision of expensive cleanliness that strode into the factory less than three hours before. His pale blue slacks and shirt were nearly the colour of the sawdust that covered the rest of the building's interior, as was his dark hair. The once sparkling white canvas shoes were as filthy with grease and grime as Marlie had expected.

He pulled off the goggles and laid them aside. His tanned skin, his dark eyebrows and deep grey eyes contrasted sharply against the beige dust on the rest of his face. He looked as if he were wearing a Technicolor mask. He grinned at the two who had been watching.

'That's some machine! That fellow should be able to do anything!'

'Well, it won't,' Howard said with an unexpected moroseness. 'Just try to get it to type.'

Greg nodded. 'Probably won't spell, either,' he suggested.

'No, it's not too good with English,' Marlie added her bit. 'It emigrated from Austria, you know.'

'That accounts for it,' Greg wiped a grimy hand across his chin and looked down at his soiled clothing. 'Do you have a place where I can wash up? I'll call a cab, but the driver would take one look at me like this and run like crazy.'

'Sure,' Howard said, rising slowly from his stool. 'Where do you have to go? Marlie and I are leaving now. Could we drop you?'

'Might be out of your way.'

'Try us and see.'

Ten minutes later, the three were crowded together in the front seat of the battered station-wagon. Both Marlie and Howard owned newer vehicles, but with the back seat folded down, the old wagon held the laundry, supplies, fishing gear, coolers and any last-minute items they decided to cart back and forth. The old car might sputter and heat up on hills, but it took the roads through the flat back areas of Virginia Beach with the slow roll of a battleship.

Marlie, sitting in the middle, kept her feet up on the hump in the floorboard, drew her knees in and tried to make herself as small as possible. She was conscious of Greg at her right, the proximity of his wide chest to her shoulder as his left arm lay across the back of the seat. She tried to concentrate on the road ahead, wishing she were not so aware of him, of his shaving lotion, of his relaxed breathing, of his aura of total masculinity.

He was naturally a large-boned person, and unused to being tightly squeezed into a small area. He lounged back, taking more than his third of the seat, as unconsciously as he took a big and successful man's share of life.

Marlie tried to keep her eyes on the road, but the rear-view mirror was in her line of vision. As she stared into it, she got a classic view of the cargo carried in the back. She doubted if Greg, with all his money, had ever ridden in anything as battered or as jumbled. He appeared unconcerned, but she wondered what he thought about it.

She kept tilting her head, curious about the route her uncle was taking. She had assumed Greg was staying in one of the luxury hotels near the beach, but they weren't heading in that direction.

Their speed was slow because the evening traffic was heavy. Summer brought vacationers to Virginia Beach from all over the country, and many parts of the world. The gulfstream, travelling reasonably close to the coast, warmed the water, and the natural gentle slope of the shore bottom was sandy with no rock or coral to cut the feet of visitors. The city gave its attention to maintaining the golden sands, keeping them clean and litter free, and going to great expense to rebuild the beaches when the occasional hurricane created havoc along the coast.

The result was an influx of holiday-makers as soon as the weather would permit, and a holiday atmosphere that continued through the summer and up until the autumn storms drove the sun-worshippers from the beach.

For many blocks in from the shore, private residences and large apartment buildings catered to the tourists, and while they might be half empty and desolate during the

winter months, during the warm part of the year they
carried an air of one huge block party.

As Howard eased his way through traffic, Marlie
savoured the atmosphere. Singly, in couples, in groups
and family parties, people strolled across and along sand-
dusted streets. They wore bathing suits or shorts, sunhats
and dark glasses. On street corners they called farewell or
suggestions for meeting later to bosom friends they had
met only that day.

The air, blowing in the open windows of the slowly
moving car seemed full of the prevailing spirit. It smelled
of ocean, sand, suntan oil, hotdogs and charcoal smoke.
Marlie watched one couple as they strolled down the
street. They alone of all the people she had seen, took no
notice of the holiday spirit. They were too caught up in
each other. Without touching, without gazing at each
other, there was an absorption about them that excluded
everything around them and left their world undisturbed.
Marlie felt a longing suddenly, and realised it was cen-
tring on the large, relaxed man at her side. Then she felt,
rather than saw him turn his head, as if he were reading
her feelings.

'I'm taking you out of your way,' he said, making casual
conversation.

Afraid he had noticed her self-consciousness, Marlie
tried to be flippant.

'Oh, are you driving from that side of the car?' Marlie
was brought up short by her own remark. She intended
to be witty, but had she sounded as shrewish to him as
she had to herself? If so, he apparently took no notice of
it.

'In a manner of speaking,' he said casually. She saw his
head turn to look over her shoulder, into the back of the

car. He shifted slightly as he reached back, but she couldn't see what he was picking up.

'Humm, a Flueger,' he mused. 'You must have good fishing out your way.'

'Some of the best in the country,' Howard replied as he made a left turn, causing Marlie to wonder where he was going. 'We're just off Back Bay, you know.'

'Bluegills,' Greg said with decision. 'I've heard they are fighting little devils.'

'We call them bream,' Howard said as he slowed for two small boys to carry a large rubber raft across the street. 'Handled right, they're good sport and good eating.'

'I thought you went for the big fish,' Marlie said, biting her tongue after her admission. She hadn't meant to say anything about seeing his picture in the paper with a record-size marlin, caught off the shore of Florida.

'Oh, there are fish and there are fish,' Greg said lazily, his grin telling her he knew exactly what was behind her remark. She bit her lip and looked ahead into the glare of the lowering sun as Greg leaned forward to speak around her.

'What test line is a fair handicap?'

Howard was silent for a moment. 'Remember what we bought last time?' he asked Marlie.

'No, but we special ordered a very light line, that I do recall.'

'Wish I could remember,' Howard sounded irritated. 'Good for bream though. They're small, but for its weight, you won't find a better fighter in the world.'

'I'd like to try them,' Greg mumbled and reached back again to turn over the box that held the Flueger reel.

Marlie hadn't heard the conversation that included

their destination, so she was surprised when they pulled into the yacht basin. Most of the boats were small cabin cruisers. At one long pier several large yachts were drawn up.

It was natural, she thought, that Greg should have a yacht, and she thought it would probably be one of the larger ones. Had he been on an ocean cruise? Then she remembered he could have been travelling the inland waterway. Not too many people knew of the continuing path through bays, canals and rivers. It allowed ships of ocean-going size to travel from New Jersey to Florida and then on to Texas protected from the elements on the ocean and the gulf.

At Greg Alston's direction, Howard drove the battered station-wagon up to the parking area at the end of the pier, and parked. Marlie had expected Greg to get out of the car as soon as he opened the door, but as it swung wide, letting in the breeze off the water, he hesitated.

'How about coming aboard for a bite to eat? I'm interested in hearing more about your freshwater fish, and I'm hungry. How about you?'

'Not dressed like this!' Marlie was firm in the face of Howard's wavering hesitancy. She, too, was hungry, but the sounds of a party could be heard from one of the other large boats, and she had visions of being compared to the beautiful Joan Owens-Lane again.

'And if I remember right, you were supposed to attend a party, right?' She put forward another reason why she felt it unwise to go aboard.

Greg shrugged, but there was a hint of obstinacy around the corners of his mouth.

'I've got other things on my mind. If you're upset about your clothes, that's a suitcase back there, isn't it? I'd feel better if I could shower and change before I ate. You could, too.'

'That suits me,' Howard said, overriding the objections Marlie planned on making. 'Are there three showers aboard? I'm for that, and I could eat a horse.'

'You'll have to settle for a seahorse, if I know my cook,' Greg said, getting out of the car. Once straight, he gave Marlie a bow. 'Just show me what you want carried on board, and I will be your own personal stevedore.'

'Oh, how the mighty have come down in the world,' Marlie said as she took the proffered hand, stepping out on to the sand-covered surface of the parking area.

During the winter, Marlie had chided herself after succumbing to the lure of a sale and buying a new set of luggage. Then it had seemed the height of the ridiculous to use an expensive set of pale blue suitcases, complete with matching dressbag just to go back and forth to the cabin on the river. Now she was glad she had spent the money. As she followed Greg Alston who carried the dressbag and weekend case on to the boat, she felt they somehow made up for her shabby appearance.

The yacht was everything she could have imagined if she had decided to dream up a luxury craft. It was probably not in the style of those owned by the legendary Greek shipowners, she reasoned, but in her opinion it was perfection. She guessed its length to be close to a hundred feet overall. In comparison with the other boats close by, it was outsized, and stood tall in the water when put against the smaller launches and the low profile of the sailing yacht moored next to it.

The gleaming white of the hull and superstructure contrasted with the dark water and the rich brown-gold wood teak of its trim. The wide fantail was designed to be glass enclosed, but when they arrived the panels had been folded back to take advantage of the evening breeze.

To Marlie, who sailed when time and opportunity permitted and was therefore used to boats being built close to the water-line, the superstructure seemed enormous. The enclosed area on the main deck was larger than many small residences. Above that was another large deck only partially filled by the wheel-house, and the captain's quarters, Marlie supposed.

The portholes in the hull were standard, but the wide square windows that looked out on to the main and upper deck were large, square, and in her opinion, far from nautical.

That same lack of shipboard flavour continued and was strengthened as they entered the salon. Formality prevaled in the guise of velvet-upholstered, high-backed easy chairs, a comfortable-looking cushion-backed sofa in a muted floral pattern and a dark green carpet that was thick and soft. The end tables and lamps could have been in any house where the owner had the taste for antiques and the wherewithal to buy the best.

The odours of diesel fuel, oil and gas that always seemed to prevail around the docks was lost once they boarded. As they passed through the salon Marlie caught a whiff of something delicious being prepared in the galley.

She followed Greg down a ladder—she reminded herself of the nautical term—though in reality it was a stair, only slightly steeper than usual. As they walked along a companionway she could see, through open doors, into the mahogany panelled staterooms. Where was that efficiently designed, but cramped style usually found aboard boats? she wondered, as she gazed into the spacious areas.

Greg led the way into the third area and laid the suitcase and dressbag on the bed.

'We're very civilised. The shower works just like any other. No strange handles to manipulate,' he said. 'See you on the deck in half an hour.'

'I'll be there,' Marlie answered and walked over to peer through the porthole. To approach her luggage would put her too close to Greg for her comfort, so she waited until he left the stateroom. Once the door was closed, she made a dash for the zippered bag, jerking the handle in her haste to get it open. Then she sighed in relief. The peach-coloured, spaghetti-strapped sundress was there. She had tried to remember, as she had been walking up the gangway, whether she had brought it or not. Her packing that morning could only be described as helter-skelter, since she had slept through her alarm clock's buzz. Dinner on a yacht had not been a part of her plans.

The shower was warm, washing away the grime and the petty problems of the day. Marlie stepped out of the stainless steel cubicle refreshed and prepared for a glorious evening.

As she wrapped a large soft towel around her body, using another to absorb the water in her hair, she smiled down at the large monogram on the towel. She wondered if her expectations for the evening were because of, or in spite of, Greg. The earlier arguments in the factory seemed a world away.

Had she really jumped on the man with both feet, as the saying went? There was no denying she had, and the memory surprised and shocked her. Had he really done anything to deserve it, or had the entire episode been her fault? Perhaps it was the result of fatigue, the heat, and her frustration when she spilled the paint.

Working in the factory might be harmful, she thought. A winter spent in a classroom with energetic eight- and nine-year-olds was a strain. The vacation she could be enjoying was being taken up by the labour in the factory as she tried to help Howard catch up on back orders. They were almost up to date, so before long she could take some time off.

She dried her hair and decided she was being dishonest in her reasoning. Nothing could make her ill-tempered and snappish unless she allowed it. If she was shrewish, she alone was at fault. The decision was hers, and there would be no more of it.

She heard the roar of a speedboat, and shortly afterwards she felt the slight movement of the deck under her feet as the ship reacted to the smaller boat's wake. It brought her out of her reverie and reminded her she was keeping two hungry men waiting.

From the zippered carry-on bag that held her few cosmetic concessions to vanity, Marlie pulled out the blow-drier and went to work on her hair. As the warm air blew across the strands, she pushed it into a page-boy that waved slightly as it fell just below her shoulders. She surveyed the effect as it gleamed back at her from the small mirror over the built-in vanity. Because of the dying light, she flipped the wall switch. In the brightness her hair glistened and looked far different from the sawdust-filled mop she sported when she first boarded the ship. Not as striking as if it were platinum blonde, she thought, but then what was? Dismissing that little envious thought, she 'did' her face with a dusting of powder, added a light touch of eyeshadow and decided to leave off both blusher and mascara. Her eyelashes were thick and surprisingly dark for one of her colouring, and with the golden tan she had been building since the summer began, the blusher was unnecessary.

From the weekend bag she took the low sandals that were no more than leather soles in which long strings were threaded through loops, criss-crossing her feet, and wrapping around her slender ankles. They showed off her well-formed feet and legs and, by careful planning, she had been able to get narrow grosgrain ribbon to match many of her outfits, including the peach-coloured dress.

A glance at her thin gold watch as she fastened it to her arm, told her she was at the end of the half an hour her host had given her. She stepped into the dress, put her things back into her bags and closed them, making them ready to be carried to the car when they left.

A last look in the mirror assured her the dress was all she had expected it to be. The close-fitting bodice over the flaring skirt showed off her feminine but not over-full figure. She was unable, in the small mirror, to check the hemline, but looking down, she was pleased with the effect of the shoes and skirt together.

All hands on deck, she told herself as she left the stateroom.

CHAPTER THREE

WHEN she arrived in the salon, she found Greg alone. All the evidence of his labour in the factory had disappeared with his shower and change of clothing. His hair was still damp, and she noticed he had combed it while it was wet, with no thought of drying or styling it. Around the edges where it had begun to dry and was free of the restrictions of comb and moisture, the waves had begun to form. She felt an unaccountable pleasure in knowing he was careless about his natural good looks.

In wine trousers with a wine-and-white-patterned shirt, he was casually dressed, but again that tailored elegance she had noticed in the factory was apparent. Still, he seemed more human. Was that because she knew him better now, because she was not shown up at a disadvantage? Possibly her more gentle feelings came about because she had decided not to allow the less attractive side of her nature to hold sway.

He had opened a glass door on a built-in bookcase, and had removed a wooden duck decoy. Marlie had noticed it as they passed through the salon earlier. It appeared to be one made, painted and antiqued in her uncle's factory but it was hard to be certain.

'One of ours?'

Greg looked up as she spoke. 'One made by your uncle. I don't know who painted it.'

Marlie stepped closer, her knowledgeable eye travelling over the markings on the wings. It was a decoy that had been made years before when the little curves that indicated the feathers had been put on with a thin brush and black stain. Now they used black, felt-tipped pens. The number of feathers indicated told her who had painted it. In the days of the brushwork, the markings had been kept to a minimum because of the time and risk involved. Only one painter had ever taken that much time with each decoy.

'Sally Marshall,' Marlie announced, remembering how Howard complained about the time Sally had put into each decoy, often making the shipments late.

'She knew how to paint ducks,' Greg replied, and the slight emphasis on the word 'she' brought Marlie to instant attention.

'Just what do you mean by that?' Marlie demanded. Her voice was sharp, made more so by the memory of chiding herself in the stateroom, accepting all the blame for the argument earlier in the day. Obviously she was wrong. He was deliberately provoking her.

A sharpness in Greg's glance indicated his surprise that she should take offence, but a mulish expression formed around his mouth, as if caught in a stance he was committed to defend. An odd humour glinted in his dark eyes.

'I didn't mean anything by that, but since the subject came up, you could take a few lessons from her technique—and her colouring. She's really very good.'

'I'm glad you like her work,' Marlie said stiffly. 'Perhaps if you speak to my uncle, he will get her back to do your work—if you're willing to absorb the cost of the time she takes.'

Marlie had been standing, her chin out, shoulders back, and eyes blazing. Greg Alston gazed down at her from the pinnacle of his superiority. She had struck an artery with her jab, that much was apparent. His voice was cold, belying what she had at first thought was a twinkle in his eyes.

'Alston's carries only the best. Our customers expect it, even if they have to pay more. I've dealt with your uncle because his work has always been superior, and on time—until now.'

Until now. Superior and on time until now? The words rang in Marlie like a fire gong. He was not only telling her she didn't know how to paint ducks, he was laying the blame for the lost shipment at her door. She took a backward step, feeling herself revert to the seven-year-old tomboy who wanted to punch her enemy in the nose.

'Sorry it took me so long,' Howard's voice from the companionway interrupted the argument. Greg Alston turned to greet Marlie's uncle with all the urbanity of a man who had been marking time by discussing the weather.

'I thought it was a woman's privilge to be late.' Marlie had tried to make her comment light, but the tremor in her voice told her astute uncle the entire story. She saw his eyes narrow for a moment before he turned his attention to their host.

'I'm glad to meet your lovely lady,' Howard said. 'She's like vintage champagne—getting better with age.'

'Is she better for the ageing, or does she just seem that way when compared to the younger generation?' Greg asked.

Marlie wondered if that, too, was some slur on her until she realised they were talking about the boat. In her state of agitation, even that bothered her. What was it with this man that he and her uncle could talk in a language all their own? It seemed they instinctively knew what the other meant, and she felt left out of the conversation.

What is the matter with you? she demanded of herself. Why are you suddenly a war, looking for a place to happen? Where was the Marlie who had a sense of humour, who was a happy young woman enjoying the labours of the factory after the brainwork of the winter? Why did she allow this man to get under her skin? He obviously didn't object to her duck painting. He had been getting her work for years as she had often helped out in the factory, so what were his complaints?

While she was wondering, Greg and Howard had been busy at a small bar. Howard handed her a glass filled with tomato juice and garnished by a stick of celery. She arched her brows, but his grin was reassuring.

'Made yours straight,' he said.

That, in their particular jargon, meant straight tomato juice, since Marlie had never developed a taste for alcohol. She took a sip and looked at the glass again. Something had definitely been added in the way of spices. The drink had a bite of its own and was delicious. Wrapping a napkin around the outside to prevent the condensation from dripping on her dress, she followed the men out on to the deck.

The sun was just dipping down behind the trees, and across the wide expanse of fresh water, the reflection rippled in wavelets of gold. The breeze, crossing the narrow strip of land that separated them from the ocean, had made the heat of the day a memory. As the glowing orb in the west slowly disappeared into a rim of brightness and then was gone, the lights of the other boats came on, glittering across the water in a multiplicity of dancing reflections.

The sounds that were somehow muffled by the day were

more noticeable in the darkness. The tinkle of ice in glasses, the well-modulated voices of people enjoying a quiet but convivial gathering drifted from the nearest boat. Farther along the pier a child was relating some experience of the day—a young voice, pitched high with excitement.

While the men discussed draft and displacement, Marlie walked to the rail and stood looking out at the reflections of the light on the water. As usual, being around water brought out a peace in her. She had often wondered if there was any truth in the theory that man, like all life, came out of the sea. Like so many other people, she had an affinity with the water that refused to be denied.

'Hey,' Howard called to Marlie. 'You can admire the view later. We're hungry.'

She turned, feeling guilty that she was keeping them from their dinner, and returned Greg's smile as he motioned her to precede him into the dining room.

Again a semi-formality prevailed. The dark wood of the furniture and walls was a contrast to the snow-white table linen, the patina of old silver, and the sparkle of the glasses. A centrepiece of daisies and yellow candles added colour.

By a buffet laden with covered dishes, stood a short, chubby man in a white steward's coat. The aroma of the food drew Marlie towards the table along with Howard and Greg. She had forgotten how hungry she was.

Even if her work hadn't given her an appetite, she would have done justice to the dinner placed before her by Henry the cook, steward, and jack of all trades, as she was soon to learn. The tossed salad was garnished with a dressing made of vinegar and oil with spices that gave it a distinctive and unusual flavour. Crabflake *au gratin* and a baked potato were followed by a strawberry torte that could have made her jealous of the cook. But she was too grateful for excellence of a meal she had not laboured to prepare. Still, she gave Henry the satisfaction of knowing her feelings.

'I'm so jealous of your skill,' she said as he removed the dishes from the table. 'Is there any chance of kidnapping you? With your permission I'll torture you for the secret of that salad dressing.'

Henry grinned and started to reply, but Greg broke in smoothly.

'Henry's knowledge he keeps to himself, but I warn you, any attempt to steal him away would be useless. I keep a guard on him night and day.'

'But what guard can stand against both determination and ingenuity? You never know how far someone will go to get what they want.'

Marlie smiled over the candles set in tall glass cylinders. She sounded brash, she knew, but she wasn't going to let him have the last word.

'That's true enough,' Greg replied, a small smile softening his face. 'But trespassers should know about paying penalties. It would depend on relative values. Is what you're after worth the risk if you're caught?'

Marlie started to retort when she realised they had left the subject of Henry and were moving towards more dangerous ground. Greg was leaning back, watching her from under half-lowered lids, the smile that played across his face was that of a predator, stalking, watching, ready to pounce. She lowered her eyes for a moment, knowing his words held a trap. She was not going to fall into it, she decided. As if it were a physical action, she was aware of his emotional balance—mentally poised, waiting to parry and return a thrust. It occurred to her that the best way to catch him totally off guard was to remove his target, leaving him nothing to fight.

'Oh, well,' she sighed, shrugging her shoulders as if in defeat. 'Henry, your dressing is good—but there's a limit to everything.'

Her victory was Greg's impatience as he crumpled his napkin, laying it by his plate.

Henry served coffee by the loungers on the rear deck. Marlie sipped the strong black brew and turned her gaze back to the lights reflected on the water. The breeze from the ocean had cooled the air. The tiny wavelets of the inland bay were breaking against the side of the boat, creating their own music. The night was clear, full of stars, and the moon was rising.

Moonlight and romance. Marlie felt the words going through her like a song. Without conscious intention, she looked over at Greg. He was deep in conversation with Howard, telling a story about a fishing trip. She watched him as he talked, noticing the absence of gestures.

The deck was lit by torches. They served the dual purpose of keeping away insects and adding atmosphere. Greg Alston, she thought, should always stay in torch-light.

The flickering illumination brought out a primitive, an almost savage quality to his naturally good looks. The planes of his face created highlights and shadows. His eyes caught and reflected the flames that seemed to come from within.

When women write love songs, he's the object of their compositions, Marlie thought. Then unbidden came a less welcome idea. Miss White-and-bright would be the counterpart they had in mind.

'Ahoy—the *Veronica*!' came a call from the dock. Marlie looked over the rail to see several people start up the gangway. Leading the group was a tall blond man who waved a bottle of champagne like a flag. Behind him came Joan Owens-Lane and two other couples.

Was it her imagination, or did Greg show some reluctance as he rose and went to greet his guests? He introduced Lyle Kearns as the man with the bottle. Mr and Mrs Caulder were a pair of physical mismatches in Marlie's opinion. He was tall and grotesquely fat while she was short and must have weighed all of ninety pounds. His eyes measured everything in terms of possible cost, because his wife's arms and fingers dripped with jewels, making them a psychological match. Marlie had not caught their first names.

Kara and Bill Holmes were two of the beautiful people, tall and slim. They were open and friendly with Greg, Joan and Lyle, but their condescending air towards the Caulders said as much about them as it did the older couple.

The six people had come from another party, it was obvious by their dress. The men were wearing dinner jackets, and the women, floor-length attire. Mrs Caulder had unfortunately chosen to wear a long-sleeved mauve caftan which not only looked out of place and uncomfortable, but her hair, which had a slight reddish tint, made it an unflattering colour.

Kara, with her dark hair in braids that looped below her ears, was exotic in a silver, backless jumpsuit. Joan too wore a jumpsuit of sorts, a white close-fitting garment that was both backless and strapless. The loose, gold gauze jacket did nothing to hide her considerable charms.

Marlie thought the baggy jacket with its long sleeves

and improbable length, it came almost to Joan's knees, would look ridiculous on anyone else. But grudgingly she had to admit Joan seemed to show up the others, Marlie included. Amazing what some women could do with style, she thought.

Joan had attached herself to Greg the moment she stepped on board, and after a sharp look of recognition at Marlie, she tightened her hold on his arm.

Marlie chided herself for that feline pleasure she felt, but it was clear in the factory that Joan had looked her over, summed her up in the light of possible competition and dismissed her. But since then, with a shower and a change of clothing, Marlie had taken a step up in the socialite's estimation. Joan clung to Greg, her voice so honey-sweet and false, Marlie wondered how he could stand it.

'Darling, I was worried about you,' she murmured just loud enough for everyone to hear. 'I was afraid you had been devoured by all those wooden ducks.'

'I was rescued just in time.' Greg's answer, Marlie noticed, showed more patient boredom than genuine interest.

Don't think like that, she warned herself. You're not in their league. She had to be practical or she was in for trouble, she knew. Still, the thought left her feeling a bit chilled and empty.

Henry appeared with more champagne and glasses. For a few minutes the guests mingled as glasses and drinks were passed about. Marlie, not at all interested in champagne, opted for another cup of coffee before the pot was removed.

Marlie had expected Joan to keep her stranglehold on Greg's arm for the entire evening, but the tall, silky Kara had other plans. She drew Joan away to the aft end of the deck with some gossip. Mrs Caulder followed. They gathered around a small table near where Marlie sat on a chaise-longue. By Joan's careful placement of her chair, so her back was between Marlie and the others, she effectively cut Marlie out of the conversation.

Between Kara and Joan, the talk was blatantly full of names often read in the papers, and Marlie noticed Mrs Caulder was also being excluded from the intimacy. She was not one to allow much of that, so she kept interrupting with titbits of information obviously gleaned from the gossip and social columns of various papers. Marlie felt sorry for the little woman, who looked winded by trying to keep pace with the others. She seemed determined to worm her way into the higher social structure.

Marlie let their verbal struggle go over her head as she looked out over the bay. The scene was still the same, the lights still danced, but the mood was lost under the hubbub on the boat. She tried to keep her mind on what she was seeing, but she was aware of the tensions surrounding the three women. Joan was tense, as if, in turning her back on Marlie, she half expected an attack. Kara was making moist circles on the little table with her glass. In little signals made up of moues and raised eyebrows, she was communicating her disapproval of Mrs Caulder to Joan. Mrs Caulder was shredding a paper cocktail napkin and chain-smoking, lighting one cigarette immediately after crushing out the one preceding it.

The men had gathered together in a huddle about ten feet away. Greg was leaning against the rail, idly turning the stem of a glass in his hand as he listened to one of Howard's fish stories. The others gave Marlie the impression they were only waiting for a chance to interrupt.

Bill Holmes was wearing a polite, patient attitude that left Marlie cold. Mr Caulder had finished assessing the cost of the boat and was inspecting the clothing of the others. Lyle Kearns was looking frankly bored.

As his eyes wandered, they met Marlie's. She gave a little shiver of apprehension when she realised she had caught his attention. She saw his face change from boredom to interest, to decision, to charm-boy on his way to make a conquest. She was reminded of the dial settings on a washing machine.

Lyle was weaving slightly as he crossed the deck and sat on the end of the chaise. Marlie drew up her feet to keep them from being trapped beneath him.

'You looked all by yourself, and I'm all by myself, so how about saying beautiful words to each other?'

'Sorry,' Marlie replied. 'There's no more room.'

He looked around, confused. 'No room for what?'

'No more room for words,' Marlie explained. 'Look around, words all over everywhere. Look at those long sentences from the fishing stores. See that marlin caught in that one?' If he thought she was a kook he might go away. No such luck. She could tell by the sudden light in his eyes he was in favour of a game, anything to break the pall of the evening.

He peered in the direction Marlie pointed. 'Yeah—but if we speak very low, maybe we can get our talk in under that group over there.' He waved a hand in the direction of an area on the other side of the deck.

'Oh, I don't think so,' Marlie argued. 'If they bunched up, ours would be pushed down into the bay, and if there is one thing I can't stand, it's soggy prose.'

Lyle nodded solemnly. Then he smiled. 'How about asking Henry to bring out a fan? We'll blow the rest away.'

'And have a breezy conversation?' Marlie asked. She gave herself ten points for a cliché.

'Fascinating!' the tall Kara said abruptly. She leaned forward, tapping Marlie on the shoulder with one long, perfectly manicured nail. 'Why haven't we seen you around before?'

'Oh, I'm around, I'm just usually busy—earning my living,' Marlie said airily. She expected that to take care of any further interest she might have received from Kara. Joan's smirk, intended to be an insult, was in fact a reward.

'Well, some people must do it, I guess,' said Mrs Caulder. She was quickly picking up on Kara's and Joan's attitudes, Marlie noticed. 'Tell me, dear, how do you occupy yourself?'

Marlie formed the words in her mind with exceptional clarity: I occupy myself by instructing the offspring of people who do not have yachts. No matter how she phrased it, she was still saying teacher. That was somehow too respectable an admission to the three snobs. They were ready to make fun, quite well-bred fun, of course, of anything she said. She wasn't about to give them her profession to shred with their perfect nails. She thought of saying she did night duty on the seamier streets in town, but that would be carrying things too far. That would embarrass both Greg and Howard. Then it occurred to her that the present truth might do as well. She looked them straight in the eyes.

'I paint ducks.'

Mrs Caulder and Kara looked blank. Joan snickered behind her napkin. Lyle parked his elbow on his knee and his chin in his hand. The alertness of his eyes proved his interest.

'How do you catch them?' he asked.

The explanation came from over Marlie's shoulder.

'With a duck catcher—it's a gun that shoots a lasso,' Howard said. 'Gal, I think we'd best be gettin' down the road a piece.'

Marlie, who was still nursing the cup of after-dinner coffee, nearly choked on a sip. Obviously from his countrified accent, Howard's reaction to the company was the same as hers. He was not the type to drawl, and he never sounded like a country bumpkin. He, too, was laying it on for their benefit. Fleetingly, Marlie thought she and Howard had a snobbery of their own. She felt justified since the others had started it, but she was willing to admit her own faults.

As she rose and turned, Marlie saw Greg standing by Howard. His mouth was grim.

'If you'll excuse me for a moment,' he said to the assembled group, 'I'll bring up Miss Richmond's bags. Miss Richmond, perhaps you'd like to come down to make sure you packed everything.'

The formality alerted her to his mood, even if she hadn't seen his grim expression. She had packed everything and she had no desire to be alone with him in his present mood. But short of refusing to go, there was little she could do. He looked angry. He didn't like the put-down she and Howard had given his friends, she was sure. But then neither she nor her uncle had asked to be included in their group. If he mentioned it, she would tell him so. She was primed for an argument when they entered the compartment.

In the stateroom she wordlessly swept her hand around to indicate nothing had been left. Then she nodded to the bags, which he ignored.

'Miss Richmond,' his voice was cold. 'I would advise you not to encourage Lyle Kearns.'

'What?' That was the last thing she expected.

'I am told I speak quite clearly. I would advise you, for your own good, to leave Lyle Kearns alone.'

A warmth spread into her cheeks, as she glowered up at him. She fought to keep her voice under control.

'Mr Alston, I have absolutely no interest in Lyle Kearns, nor in anyone else at the moment.' She paused and took a deep breath. She had a lot to say. 'If I did, I hardly see how it could be any concern of yours. You purchase a product made in my uncle's factory. Our responsibility to you stops with giving you a satisfactory product. Yours ceases with payment. If I choose to interest myself in anyone, including Mr Kearns, I need neither your advice nor your permission. Is that perfectly clear, Mr Alston?' Marlie took a deep breath. Under the circumstances, she was rather proud of herself.

Greg's answer was to step forward suddenly, catching her up in his arms. She was surprised into immobility as his lips came down on hers. Her first inclination was to fight, and she pushed at his shoulders, but his response was to hold her tighter. Her breathing became difficult, but the restriction was within her. She was aware of his strength, and his repression of it—it pulsed in his hands, and his heart within his hard chest beat against her as she was trapped by his arms.

His tongue, seeking entry between her lips, touched tender places, sending thrills racing through her. His hands, hot against her back communicated their own messages of desire.

Her mind fought his insolence, the arrogant supposition that she would welcome his advances, but her body instinctively recognised in him the source of a fulfilment long desired, and she warmed and trembled at his touch. She had ceased struggling, and her arms were moving to wrap around his back, when he suddenly released her.

She stumbled back against the bulkhead, staring at him.

'Miss Richmond—' His voice was maddeningly calm. 'Concerning those persons in whom I interest myself, both my advice and permission are needed.'

He picked up the bags and left her standing with her mouth open. He had disappeared down the hall when she closed it with a snap. Her eyes narrowed. Her voice was almost a whisper as she spoke into the empty passage way, but it held the emotions of a scream.

'You—you—oh, am I going to fix you!'

CHAPTER FOUR

As the sound of Greg Alston's footsteps receded, Marlie stood in the stateroom. She could feel the warmth in her cheeks, the pulsing of blood in her veins. Desire and anger were both passions, and one, the other, or both would show in her face if she went on deck right then. She hurried to the small but well-equipped bath and dampened a face-cloth, holding it against her flaming cheeks. The mirror showed she had achieved some results, but not enough. There was nothing she could do about the sparkle in her eyes.

'Stop that,' she ordered, but the blue eyes that stared back at her showed an obstinate desire to retain the feelings she was trying desperately to hide.

Not wanting to face that mirror any longer, she went back into the stateroom and looked around. She had better make sure she had left nothing behind. No way was she coming back after any forgotten articles. The smooth spread on the bed, the top of the built-in dresser were bare of her belongings, but she was a creature of habit. Could she have dropped something in a drawer—a comb, a brush, the soiled clothes she had worn in the factory? No, she remembered packing them in a plastic bag to keep the sawdust from getting on her clean clothes.

Sure now that she had indeed packed everything, and hoping her experience with Greg would not show on her face, Marlie left the stateroom, closing the door behind her. Her thoughts were in a turmoil. She absently bid good night to the six people who were on the deck and hurried down the gangway and over to the car. Greg had been leaning over, his arms braced against the window while talking to Howard, who was already behind the wheel. Before he could come around to assist her, Marlie was in her seat with the door closed.

He returned to Howard's window, bending down to look in at her. 'I enjoyed our dinner,' he said with a half-smile. 'We'll have to do it again sometime.'

Was that a put-down for her rudeness? Marlie wasn't sure.

'The pleasure was ours,' she answered through lips unaccountably tight and pursed. Ordering herself to behave normally was becoming increasingly unsuccessful.

He stepped back away from the car as Howard gave a wave and started the engine. As Howard backed the car and turned it slowly, the lights illuminated the side of the yacht. The white hull and superstructure stood out beautifully against the starlit night, a vision from a modern fairy-tale. For the first time, Marlie noticed the name of the ship. The *Veronica*. Another woman in his life, Marlie thought.

Marlie noticed none of the traffic on the busy highway along the ocean. When they turned off on the series of country roads that wove through the back areas of Virginia Beach, she stared out into the darkness, not seeing the lights from occasional subdivisions that became less frequent.

Some miles farther on they left the suburbs behind and drove through farming country. The car lights showed long straight rows of growing crops. The green plants stood out against the rich black earth. Through the windows of the car came the scent of fertile black soil that had been recently disturbed by a cultivator, the summer scent of dust warmed by the sun and left to cool in the evening. Occasionally she caught the perfume of honeysuckle where the fast-growing blooming weed had begun to wind itself along a fence.

The lighted windows were farther apart as they passed farmhouses, each set back from the road, usually surrounded by huge dark trees whose size indicated how long those large farms had been in existence.

Howard turned off the state route and drove along the smaller, private road that led to the river. The Norvels, who owned most of the road had opted to keep the timber on their land in preference to farming. Instead, they sold off small portions to select people for the building of fishing cabins, and ran a large camp-ground and fishing dock.

The road was dark, overhung by the wood that encroached up to the pavement, and Howard slowed, careful not to drive too fast. Sometimes the children from the camp-ground wandered through the woods and appeared suddenly out of the darkness.

Marlie's mind was neither on the drive, nor wary because of the children. Her thoughts were still back aboard the yacht.

Veronica. The name was beautiful, musical, it rolled off the tongue. She was probably a beautiful woman, Marlie thought, if the yacht had been called after her. There would be a real Veronica somewhere. And whoever she was, Marlie thought, she was probably more important in Greg Alston's life than Joan Owens-Lane.

Marlie's cheeks began to burn again. Suddenly she wished she hadn't been in such a hurry to get in the car. She wished she had stood right there on the dock and

demanded to know what kind of man he was. He had Miss
White-and-bright on his arm one minute, was kissing her
the next. Why the man was a Bluebeard!

She wriggled in her seat, angry with herself that she had
wasted a single thought on him. Remembering how
pleased she was that he had given so little attention to
Joan on the boat was enough to make her anger flare up
again.

Let that teach you, she told herself. Mind your business, and don't think about him any more.

Consciously, she gave herself a stiff lecture. Some per-
verse little thought kept trying to intrude, saying, now
here's what we'll do when we see him again.

'Marlie Richmond, you're impossible.' She had spoken
aloud before she realised it.

'I've known that for years,' Howard replied. 'What
brought on that sudden realisation?'

'Never mind,' Marlie snapped. 'You can either pull in
at Frank's, or you'll do without breakfast in the morning.'

'Oh, oh. Messed up your schedule, huh?' She saw
Howard's grin by the light of the dashboard. Marlie
turned her face to the darkness wondering why her uncle
would find that so funny.

The flurry of grocery shopping in Frank's Grocery, the
little back-country store, and the hurried activity in unloading the car at the cabin, pushed Greg to the back of
her mind. Usually they arrived at the waterway early
enough so that the weekly chore of moving in was finished
before dark. In good weather they took the lawn chairs
from the storage shed and enjoyed sitting by the water
until time for bed. They maintained a schedule of early
rising on the river.

Marlie finished her unpacking, pushing Howard to

help, and was glad to crawl between the cool sheets of her bed. She seldom had any trouble sleeping because her days were full of activity. The difference in teaching and working with her hands left her with an almost pleasant fatigue. But that night sleep fought her. She tossed in her bed, knowing she was tired, but when that pleasant drowsiness stole over her, back would come Greg's face. Most often it was accompanied by Joan Owens-Lane's platinum-blonde head at his shoulder.

She turned over and mauled her pillow, not sure if she was using it for an effigy of Greg or Joan. The socialite was never going to be her best friend, but Marlie kept insisting to herself that she disliked Greg just as much. He had one woman clinging to his arm, and yet he was finding the chance to kiss another in the stateroom. That was, she thought, a little too much, especially when that second woman was Marlie Richmond.

She was surprised by the effect of that kiss. The memory of it was still on her lips, she could still feel his hands on her back as if he had branded himself on her body, a body that had turned traitorous in its desire, and was not obeying her conscious commands to forget him. Marlie's mind fought the war of her unbidden thoughts versus her common sense until sleep came.

Even though she had been late getting to sleep, Marlie awakened early the next morning. Before dawn she was up, dressed, and had made a pot of coffee. As the light grew in the sky she watched it from her favourite spot, a large stump that had been carefully sawn to her specifications. Years before, a huge old oak tree had shaded the cabin, but lightning had destroyed her tree, so the caretaker had the stump cut at two levels. The lower one was two feet from the ground, and the upper, eighteen

inches higher, making a chair that Marlie had painted
to keep the raw wood from rotting away. For the past
three years she had made early spring trips to the river,
planting marigolds and zinnias around the base. Her
labours had produced a colourful garden around the
rustic seat.

To Marlie, the best part of the day was its beginning.
She preferred to come out to her stump while night still
held sway. At first, the world seemed not to notice the faint
grey streaks in the sky, but little by little it became aware.
A faint breeze came alive. It brought movement among
the leaves of the trees, the pussywillows on the river bank
and the grass, as if the plants themselves were stretching
towards the faint light.

She heard the flutters of little feathered wings and single
uninspired chirps among the birds, as if they enjoyed their
sleep and protested its end. The flowers at her feet were
only shadowed caricatures of themselves when she first
arrived, but they seemed to grow in colour as if freshly
painted by the day. Then the birds, cheerful little fellows
when once awake, flew down and hopped around, looking
for their first food of the day.

As the light grew, she could see, along the river, the
other cabins, and around the bend the dock where the
campers could rent boats or launch their own. The camp
itself was out of sight in the trees. The rustic cabins, set a
good distance apart, and their mowed yards were all that
intruded on nature. The waterway that lay dark and quiet
in the growing light, was originally a river, and Marlie
supposed it had been shallow at one time. Years before it
had been dredged and was now a part of the inland
waterway, where even some ocean-going ships could
travel along its course. Her head was turned to watch the

lightening of the water, so the voice startled her.

'Venus rose from the waves. I can't remember who rose from the flowers.'

Marlie looked over her shoulder to see Greg standing nearby, a fishing rod and a tackle box in his hands.

'A duck painter,' Marlie said, putting her cup on the upper plateau of the stump that served as both seat-back and table. She pushed down the elation that tried to spring up inside her and eyed his fishing equipment critically. 'You look loaded for—birdwatching?' There was no line on his reel.

He laughed. 'Howard said he could supply me with the right line to fish for bream. Not many sports shops open this early.'

'No,' Marlie bit back a laugh. His term, sports shop conjured up a vision of carpeting, fancy equipment, and enthusiastic clerks who sold specialised equipment at outrageous prices. In the vicinity of the waterway and back bay, he would find only general stores that sold everything from fishing equipment to eggs, milk and cornplasters. Two still had old-fashioned pot-bellied stoves. Her grin refused to remain hidden.

'No, our local—sports shop—doesn't open until seven.'

The flash in his eyes said he knew he had made a mistake.

Um-m—caught with your jet set showing, Marlie thought. But though he was casually dressed, everything about him said socialite, or that he was a step above the average. He was wearing what she thought might be termed designer jeans, the type never advertised on television. The pale grey knitted shirt needed no appliqué on the front to announce its quality. Such gimmicks only announced they sought the status Greg Alston took for granted.

He was wearing blue canvas deck-shoes and carried a denim jacket over his arm.

Still, he wasn't relying on his money to carry him through, she thought. She watched him strive for something to take her attention away from his thoughtless remark. He was saved by Howard who banged the door to the screened porch as he came out, carrying the coffee pot and two cups.

'Found the place, I see,' Howard held out a cup which Greg took.

'Either that, or he got lost in our direction,' Marlie said as she reached for her cup, irritated that Howard had said nothing about Greg's intended visit. Yet he had certainly known about it, if he had offered to supply Greg with a fishing-line.

Except for Marlie's stump, there were no seats on the lawn. Neither she nor Howard had had time to bring out the folding aluminium chairs they used in the yard. Howard squatted, one foot under him, the other slightly in front to balance himself.

'Pull up a chair', Howard said. Knowing her uncle as well as she did, she knew Greg was being tested. The good opinion Howard had formed of the man in the shop had been offset on the boat by his choice of friends.

She returned to her seat on the stump, watching the wealthy socialite out of the corner of her eye. Greg imitated Howard, appearing to be as at ease as any farmer taking a rest between ploughing.

'You mean sit on my fist and rear back on my thumb?' Greg asked.

'Lord, I haven't heard that one in a hundred years,'

Howard laughed. 'Had breakfast?'

Marlie knew Greg had passed with honours. She wondered if she was happy or sorry.

'Now why should I have breakfast?' Greg looked at Marlie over the top of his coffee cup. 'I thought I was invited for—let's see—if I remember right it was good Virginia ham, fresh tomatoes and the best home-made biscuits east of the Pecos?'

'Naw,' Howard shook his head 'Don't give the girl a swelled head. Doubt if she could outdo anybody past the Mississippi.'

Greg sighed. 'Well, I'll just have to rough it, I guess.'

'Thanks!' Marlie leaned over, pouring her remaining coffee into a bare spot in the flower bed. 'That's why you made sure I bought that ham last night, but you didn't see fit to tell me we were having biscuits for breakfast.' She stood up, shoving both hands in the pockets of her jeans. 'You can forget the best fishing, I haven't turned on the oven.' She strode off towards the cabin, and not until she entered the kitchen did she remember the coffee cup sitting on the stump.

She called to Howard from the window.

'Bring in my cup and some tomatoes when you come!' She hoped there were tomatoes on the vines. But she wasn't going to be embarrassed if there weren't. Howard had promised them, not she. He sometimes forgot the terrapins had a feast when they could reach a ripe one. Working quickly, Marlie flipped on the oven, set the table and laid out what she needed to prepare breakfast. She cooked the way she had been taught by her mother who had been schooled by her own mother, and she swiftly sifted the selfraising flour into a large bowl, putting in more than she would usually do for the bread she was making.

She had sprayed her bread pan, made a depression in the flour and was adding the milk, salt, baking-powder and shortening when Greg strolled into the kitchen. He was carrying the coffee pot in one hand, and the handles of the three cups were hooked over the fingers of the other.

'Howard went tomato hunting,' he said, putting his load on the counter. With his head cocked to one side, he watched as Marlie, using her right hand, mixed the ingredients for the biscuits.

He leaned against the counter, supporting part of his weight on his left elbow and forearm. He was too tall for his stance, so his left knee was bent, and Marlie was aware of its closeness. The faint elusive scent of his aftershave was a brand unfamiliar to her, but then it would be, she supposed. There was something persuasive about it, very understated, yet it created its own undercurrents. Was it the brand, or him? she wondered.

She was terribly aware of his closeness, his arm lying casually on the counter, the muscles of his forearm swelling slightly with the strain of holding his own weight.

His eyes were moving from her hands, working with the dough, to her face. She was aware of their gaze, and though she couldn't be sure, she felt a tingling along her side as if her body had been lightly touched by his appraising look.

What was he thinking? she wondered. After experiencing Henry's gourmet cooking, she thought he would probably find hers countrified. Worried about it, she jumped to her own defence before she was struck.

'Like it or not, I make bread by an old family custom,' she said airily. 'For more than a hundred years—I guess a hundred and thirty now—' She paused, wondering about the story and its age. 'Anyway, since my great-great-grandmother's time, we have always made bread the same way.'

'Sounds like some story,' Greg said, shifting his weight. Was it her imagination, or did he move closer?

'A family legend,' Marlie replied. 'Years ago, my great-great-grandmother's family had a small farm. The land wasn't too good, the crops had been bad, and they were very poor.' Her voice slipped into the dreamy tone she used with her class that kept them spellbound when she told them stories.

'Some miles away there was a very rich man who was getting on in years, and he decided it was time to take a wife. He was a very handsome man—he was said to ride a white horse.' She raised her eyebrows as she glanced at Greg.

'That may or may not be true about the horse. Well, he started visiting all the families in the area, looking for a young wife. Naturally she had to be able to cook, so he would arrive just before dinner-time and watch the noon meal being prepared. Oh, I forgot to mention that he was a man who hated waste.'

The dough was the right consistency, so Marlie, using a little of the excess flour, rubbed her hands to clean off the clinging dough and started forming the biscuits by hand. From long practice she knew just how much to pinch off each time to get them uniform. She was acutely aware of Greg's closeness as he watched. To take her mind off him she continued with her story.

'Most people roll their dough out on boards and cut their biscuits with a cutter, or, barring that, the top of a drinking glass will do. Then they take the scraps and reform, roll and cut again. But you can only reroll once and then the bread gets tough, so the last scraps are usually thrown away. Well, the wealthy old gentleman didn't like that.'

'He thought it was wasteful,' Greg said.

Marlie nodded. 'He kept riding his horse down the road until he reached my great-great-grandmother's house. I told you they were poor—so poor they didn't have a breadboard, a rolling pin, or even a biscuit cutter—'

'And they had no glasses, they were drinking out of Mason jars,' Greg added. Marlie gave him a speculative look. Was he making fun of her? No, he seemed to be interested.

'Exactly. So when my great-great-grandmother made her biscuits, she shaped them by hand. Of course there was no waste, and the wealthy man had found his wife. That's the way customs begin, I guess. Anyway, since that time we've always made our biscuits by hand.'

'Any white horses on the horizon?'

His question caught Marlie by surprise. She looked up to see his wide grin and the amusement in his eyes.

What have I done? she demanded of herself. How could she repeat that old tale to him, a wealthy bachelor, sought-after by women from all over the country? He had to be thinking Howard, too, was following in the old customs, bringing him home to see the daughter of the house at work in the kitchen.

Knowing what he must be thinking, mortification caused her to want to sink through the floor. She felt the scalding blush rise to her cheeks. She threw up a hand in an attempt to hide it.

Greg laughed and handed her a paper towel.

'You do wear the strangest things on your face,' he said.

Marlie looked down at her hands, covered with flour. She didn't have to see a mirror to know what she had done. She glared up at him, so perfectly groomed, his attire so spotless, and wondered what it was about him that made her seem so ridiculous in his presence.

The sheer impotency of her anger caused her to tremble. While he stood grinning she jerked the paper towel from his hand and threw it on the floor.

'Oh-h-h!' she squealed, stomped one plimsoll-shod foot and raced out of the kitchen.

Five minutes later, with clean face and hands, Marlie re-entered the empty kitchen. Had her outburst disgusted Greg Alston so that he had decided to leave? she wondered. Before she had time to worry or consider whether or not she was in favour of it, she heard his voice outside as he talked to Howard. The hum of the well pump and the splash of water accompanied their voices.

Marlie had the thick slices of ham sizzling in the pan, and was just sliding the biscuits in the oven, when Howard and Greg came in, each carrying two large tomatoes.

'Beefsteaks,' Howard was saying. 'You don't find them in the stores, they don't grow in the pretty shapes the housewives like to buy, but just wait until we cut into them.'

While Howard sliced tomatoes, Marlie heated another skillet and broke half a dozen eggs into the pan. By the time they had cooked to picture perfection, the ham, the tomatoes and the biscuits were on the table.

Marlie was anxious about how she was going to face Greg over breakfast, but with Howard at the table, she need not have worried. While she ate and considered what to put in their lunch, Howard swung the conversation over to where they would go on their day-long expedition.

The sides of the waterway were pocked with small widened areas where the current of the river had once meandered, creeks entered, and in many places the fish abounded.

Greg seemed to be giving Howard his entire attention, but twice she saw his gaze travel in her direction, and his knee, under the table, rested very close to hers. Twice she tried to move her feet, but that was a mistake. He shifted, too, and his leg came close again, not quite touching. She could feel the warmth, the brush of his trouser leg. He left her just that fraction of room to make any complaints foolish, yet he didn't allow her to forget his presence.

Marlie kept her eyes lowered to her plate, but she couldn't help seeing his strong arms as they moved at his side, his hands on the table when he paused to speak. The fingers of his left hand slowly rubbed the edge of the plate, bringing to Marlie the memory of those same hands as he had caressed her back the night before. She nearly choked on the ham and gave up trying to eat. She wondered if he had any idea what he was doing to her, but of course he did, she thought. Wasn't he supposed to have women up to his ears? She fought back her feelings and rose from the table.

'Excuse me, but if you're going fishing today, I'd better get your lunch ready,' she said. Efficiency, that was the game. Keep herself busy until he was safely away. She started taking bread, meat, tomatoes and lettuce from the refrigerator. She stopped to eye what she put on the counter. The one thing she was not going to do was touch anything that would get her hands dirty. Not while Greg Alston was in the cabin.

'You mean you're not going with us?' Howard asked,

when she saw them off at the boat.

'That's exactly what I mean,' Marlie answered, looking back at her garden. 'There comes the time in every gardener's life when she has to weed, and this weekend is it. You have a good time, and I'll do my thing around here.'

Was that disappointment in Greg's eyes. She pushed down the little pang she felt in herself. All he wanted was someone to tease. He might be the great Greg Alston, but even he would think twice about trying to make a fool out of Howard. But Greg was used to having flunkeys around, someone who played the fool, to make him look good in comparison, she thought. Well, let him find someone else. She wasn't hiring on to be the crew and the joker.

'You have a good time,' she said lightly, 'and I warn you, I'm planning on having fish for dinner. If you don't bring it, you don't eat.'

She stood on the grass and gave the boat a shove with a pole they kept for that purpose. Before it had drifted out into water deep enough to start the outboard motor, she had turned back towards the cabin.

Behind her she heard a sputter and a roar. She turned to wave as the bow of the fourteen-foot aluminium boat rose. The seventy-five horsepower outboard motor brought the stern down almost to the surface as the propeller bit into the water.

The boat wasn't out of sight before Marlie regretted her decision. Why had she decided to remain on the shore, when she could be out with them, enjoying what she came to do? She loved to fish, she hated pulling weeds in the garden.

Greg Alston was the reason. If it hadn't been for him, she would be with Howard. In minutes they would be sitting in the shade of some overhanging tree branches, revelling in nature as it was supposed to be. Weeding around hybrid vegetables and flowers just didn't do it.

It was all Greg Alston's fault. She looked back at the river that was silent again after their departure.

'Use him for the anchor!' she shouted after the departed boat.

CHAPTER FIVE

ONCE the breakfast dishes were washed and dried, Marlie attacked the garden. Her mood required vengeance, and every weed became Greg Alston. She usually dreaded the chore of tugging them out by the roots, but with the socialite playboy in mind, she ran out of offending plants before she had expended her energy.

Marlie's patch of garden would have fitted in a medium sized room. The purpose of the small plot was not principally the growing of vegetables, but to give her a use for other frustrations. She thoroughly enjoyed working with the soil in the early spring, and the planting. She came out on weekends as soon as the danger of frost had passed, using the labour as a release for the frustrations of a school-room full of active eight- and nine-year-olds. Third graders were rewarding to teach, but when the warm days began, and the youngsters were feeling they had spent half their lives in that classroom, they became restless and unruly. Marlie used the planting as an emotional release and spent the rest of the summer wishing she had taken up jogging.

To Howard's remarks that other emotional releases were less work and more rewarding, she turned a deaf ear. When he was persistent, she retorted that if he had wanted grandchildren, he was supposed to start with his own kids first.

'Rather have the fun and not the responsibility,' he always answered.

To her accusations that he set one standard for himself and another for her, he refused to listen. To him, women were supposed to be married to be happy. In his mind, the same wasn't true for men. When she reminded him that for every married woman there had to be a married man, he usually remembered something that needed doing, and that something effectively removed him from the conversation.

Since she had her own apartment in the city, Howard was not aware of her romantic life. Most of it was too bland to make good conversation, she thought wryly. Thomas Carson, the new assistant principal had been very attentive, but she was aware that their relationship was, at best, just a convenient pairing off between two single people at social affairs involving the other teachers. Occasionally they went to a movie or a concert. The intervals between those dates had been lengthening since she had made it plain she had no romantic interest in Thomas.

That's what I need, she thought. I need a handsome hunk to build my ego after Mr. Corporation.

The weeding done, she marched in the house and turned out three cabinets, going from them to her closet which was almost filled with the debris of clothing she had ruined at the factory, or puttering around the outboard motors when she stood by as assistant for Howard's mechanics.

While she was packing some ruined shirts in a bag to use at the factory for paint rags, she looked in the mirror.

Greg was certainly right. She did wear strange things on her face. A smudge of dust or dirt ran down her cheek and across her chin. If Howard and Greg returned early from fishing he would be laughing at her again. She looked at her watch, unable to believe not only the morning, but half the afternoon had passed. She rushed the bag of old shirts out to the station-wagon so that they would not be forgotten in the flurry of Sunday night packing.

The next two hours she devoted to Marlie. A long shower, complete with shampoo and a home hair treatment, she followed by a manicure, sorely needed after her struggle with the weeds. She eyed her choice of clothes in the closet, settling on a pair of light blue gaberdine trousers and a silk shirt which was the same shade as her trousers with the darker flowers, cunningly appliquéd, matching her eyes. Her make-up was subdued, with only the faintest eyeshadow and blusher. In a spirit of fun, she put her hair up in the two cocker spaniel ears.

That, she decided, would offset any ideas Greg might have that she was interested in him. What female, when she was after a man, would risk looking like a kid, and an unfashionable one at that?

She surveyed herself in the mirror, liking the effect, but not quite satisfied. A slight darkening of the eye shadow, as well as a little blusher added to the chin, helped to bring her face into focus and detract from the hair flopping over her ears.

The general idea, she reminded herself, was to make him think she wasn't making herself attractive for him. If she could do it without his knowledge—she slammed her hairbrush down on the dresser. Why were thoughts about that man governing her every action? She stalked off to the kitchen, promising herself she was not going to think about him again.

After a few minutes of banging cabinet and refrigerator doors, she set out the ingredients for cornbread. If Howard and Greg came back with a string of fish—and knowing Howard, they would—her uncle was going to expect another family favourite. Greg's opinion of what they called 'fish bread' was not going to matter.

Fish bread was a misnomer. None of the ingredients had anything to do with fish. It was her standard recipe with whole kernels of corn cooked in the batter. The secret of making it the way Howard liked was in heating the heavy iron skillet on the top of the stove, adding enough oil so that the round flat cake would come out cleanly when done, and sprinkling a few grains of cornmeal into the greased skillet. The batter, when poured in the pan, sizzled, giving the bottom and sides a crust that could be achieved no other way.

With the batter waiting on the back of the stove, Marlie mixed up a crisp green salad and stored it in the refrigerator. Outside, she placed the folding aluminium chairs in the shade, and put fresh wood in the open fire pit that was surrounded by a low stone wall.

When the sun was out of sight behind the trees, she lit the fire and was relaxing with a glass of iced tea when the boat came around the bend in the river.

She raised her glass in greeting. She was ready for the fish fry, her preparations standing by. There was nothing else for her to do, and her hands were clean. This time she was ready for Greg Alston, and there was going to be nothing on her face but make-up.

Because of the large boats that travelled the waterway, and the experiences of their neighbours, Marlie and Howard had eschewed a dock. Instead they had installed a slip cut into the bank, and just large enough to hold their two boats.

When Howard cut the motor and let the boat drift into the slip, Greg jumped out and tied the bow line to the cedar post that had been driven deep into the bank for that purpose.

'Do we eat, or do we starve?' Marlie called out.

'We eat! Boy, do we eat!' Howard called back, holding up a string of fish, four of which were freshwater bass.

'Did you tell our guest the rules?' Marlie asked as they walked over to the chairs by the fire.

'Sounds like I'm in for something,' Greg commented.

'Oh, I don't know,' Marlie replied. 'The rule around here is, you clean what you catch. Are you responsible for much of that string?'

Howard laughed as Greg shook his head in defeat.

'Can't win for losing. Okay,' he got to his feet. I'm starving, so I better get to cleaning.'

Marlie sat back, watching the two men as they walked across the yard. Howard paused to pick up the end of the hose as they disappeared around the end of the cabin. While they were out of sight, she slipped into the kitchen, turned on the oven for her bread and gathered the plates, glasses and silverware to set the table. A table-cloth and a clear sheet of plastic completed here load.

When the men reappeared, she was again seated, but the battered round table was covered with a gay cloth on which daffodils rose from the circular hem. The bright yellow dishes and green glasses and napkins kept up the motif. Over the set table Marlie had spread a clear plastic cloth to protect it from dust and insects.

It was Howard's time in the kitchen. He had his own secrets for the fish batter, and Marlie was never allowed to watch the preparation. Since his recipe came from Marlie's mother, she knew exactly what he did, but it was their joke that he had a well-kept secret and she pretended to go to great lengths to discover it.

Greg had accompanied Howard into the cabin, but he came out first, carrying a pitcher of tea and the big old three-legged skillet that was the star of their outdoor fish fries.

Marlie sat back watching him as he put the skillet down by the fire and raised the protective plastic, putting the pitcher of tea safely in the middle of the table.

She found it amazing that he had been out in the small boat all day, since not a wrinkle showed in his clothing nor had he a mark on the white rubber that bordered his blue deck-shoes.

Howard must have done all the work, she thought, and decided that was uncharitable. After all, what had there been to do? The boats were both watertight, the motors recently serviced, but it bothered her that she had had to work at looking clean and fresh, whereas he seemed to stay that way with no effort.

'How did you like our kind of fishing?' she asked.

'I didn't know you had a patent on it,' Greg raised his eyebrows.

'I just meant, you usually go in for larger quarry,' Marlie said. He was putting her in the wrong again.

'Anything can be a challenge,' he said. 'Some take brute force, others require a more delicate touch.' Something in his eyes told her he wasn't only discussing fishing.

Determined not to let him outpace her, but equally sure she did not want to be the loser in a battle of wits, Marlie sought an answer.

'I suppose you mean it's a matter of judgment, knowing when all your resources will be needed, and when you're having to limit yourself to the abilities of your adversary?'

His eyes flickered. She had put him in a dangerous position, and she knew it. With a smile, she sat back sipping her tea. As if stalling for time, Greg rose and walked to the table, where he poured himself a glass.

When he returned to his chair, the slight lifting at the side of his mouth caused Marlie to tense. He had worked his way out of trouble, she knew.

'Is it the abilities of my adversary that keep me in place, or how important I consider my goal?'

Marlie was glad Howard chose that minute to shout for help. As usual Greg had turned the tables on her, and it was she who needed the respite.

With his dish of batter, the plate of fish, and his cooking utensils, Howard had more than he could manage, so Marlie helped him carry his load. When they returned to the fire, his enthusiastic comments as he heated the skillet and battered the fish prevented Marlie from having to answer Greg.

Before long, the aroma from the pan was competing and winning over the pleasant smell of burning pine wood. Marlie sat back away from the heat and watched the two men as they argued over the best way to turn the fish, and how brown they should be allowed to get. They had developed a rapport during the day, and it was carrying over into the evening. No professional cook would give so much attention to each individual piece.

Marlie had put the bread in the oven when she had been in the kitchen, and her timing was perfect. The hot fish and bread, the cold salad and tea contrasted just enough for a delicious meal.

She polished off one small fillet of bass and next chose the bream. Fighting the bones of the small fish was a small price to pay for the succulent taste.

'Between the two of you, you really did a job on these fish,' she said as she wiped her fingers on her napkin. The platter that had been heaped with golden pieces was nearly empty. Both Greg and Howard had worked up an appetite, and Marlie had completely overlooked having lunch, which accounted for her hunger.

'No thanks to him,' Howard said, pushing aside a golden piece to look for one that had been cooked longer and was darker in colour. 'If I had let him have his way, they'd be raw.'

'He doesn't know the difference between browning and burning,' Greg retorted.

Marlie smiled at the camaraderie that had sprung up between them. With the difference in their backgrounds, they seemed unlikely to become friends, but apparently that hadn't stopped them.

Dusk was turning to darkness, and the glass-protected candles Marlie had put on the table were giving out a soft glow. From the marshy area across the river came the melody of the frogs. Each of the amphibians had a tone and rhythm of his own, and moved from chorus to descant in an ever changing symphony. From higher ground, the crickets added their share of sound. To the rest was suddenly added another, a human voice.

'I assume you're home, since I can see you— Should I ask if you're in to company?' Marlie didn't have to turn to know Doris Farmer was approaching. For as long as Marlie could remember, Doris and her husband had lived in a fishing cabin on the waterway. Sam Farmer had been dead for ten years, but she had stayed by the water, often fishing off the bank or taking her boat out alone. Though Marlie had known Doris most of her life, the older woman was principally Howard's friend. They were both in their fifties, both settled in their life-styles, and could be companionable without any emotional strings attached.

'You certainly should ask,' Howard called, rising from his place at the table. 'Come on over and have a glass of—' He leaned over, looking in the empty pitcher. 'Have a glass of fish.'

'Just the thing after a hard day,' Doris said as she strolled up. She gave Greg, who had risen at her approach, a critical once-over. Howard made the introductions, and Doris held out her hand. 'Well, thought we were never going to get you down here, young man.'

Marlie blinked with surprise. What was Doris talking about? Certainly they had not worked for months to bring Greg to the cabin, nor anyone else. Then she remembered that Howard had, in his efforts to push Marlie into a romance, often suggested that she invite Tom Carson out for the weekend. Possibly Doris had confused the names.

Howard was getting a chair for Doris, and she was turned away from the table, telling him some story, so neither of them saw Greg stiffen.

Marlie noticed, and wondered why it bothered him so much to be mistaken for someone else. Was it simply a matter of pride, that the great Greg Alston could not be mistaken for an inferior being, or did he resent being coupled with Marlie, even in an honest mistake?

She was still more concerned with Greg's reaction. He had said on the boat that he was interested, but what did that mean? Not much, she reasoned, not with glamorous women like Joan Owens-Lane hanging on his arm.

He was a man of pride, she knew, because she had pricked it a couple of times. That wouldn't account for his reaction. No, she decided, it was something else entirely. Doris had made the remark so casually that anyone who didn't know, would assume Marlie was involved in a lasting relationship. That was what had bothered Greg.

Where he interested himself, as he had put it, he wanted unencumbered ground, but she reminded herself that he was just camping, not building.

The idea nettled Marlie. Well, here he would find a no trespassing sign, she decided. She pushed back her chair and rose.

'Fine thing, inviting someone to tea when there isn't any,' she said to Howard. 'I'll go make another pitcher.'

'Oh, leave it and let me do it,' Doris said as she, too, stood up. 'I've been sitting in my boat all day, and I want to stretch my legs. Come on, Howard, you and I will clean up and let the youngsters go for a walk.' She leaned over, giving Greg a broad wink. 'That little dirt road out there is pretty in the moonlight.'

'Then that's for me,' Greg said promptly. He took Marlie by the arm. 'The only thing wrong with your cornbread is where it will settle if we don't walk it off.' As he started around the side of the cabin, he propelled her along by his side.

'If there was anything wrong with the bread, you didn't have to eat half of it,' she protested.

'Oh, but I did. Mustn't let the cook think I didn't appreciate it.'

Once they reached the road, Marlie tried to steer him to the left, where a quarter of a mile away, the lights of Frank's Grocery seemed safe, if a little shoddy in comparison to the places Greg spent his time. But he had ideas of his own, and he turned right. Marlie tried to object. Doris Farmer's house was the nearest in that direction, and it was a good three miles away.

The full moon illuminated the hard-packed dirt road as it ran between the shadows of the overhanging trees. The air was warm and soft with the scent of life and decay that made up the woods. A slight breeze from the south carried the smell of fresh-cut grass and the aroma of a barbecue in progress.

Suddenly Marlie was half afraid of being alone with Greg. The night was out of a romatic novel, and he made the perfect hero. Unsafe, her conscious mind warned her. Delightful, her senses said in return. A good conversation was the least dangerous course, she decided. Keep him talking. If necessary, get him into an argument, but stay safe—enjoy. Marlie decided there was something wrong with her. All this splitting of thought was unusual for her. Something else for which Greg was to blame. She never argued with herself when she was with Tom.

'Pretty back in here,' Greg said. 'When you see it from the waterway, you have no idea what's behind those trees.'

'More trees, fields and houses,' Marlie replied. 'Our part of the country is not much different from the rest, I guess.'

Greg turned his head, looking down at her. 'There are differences,' he said. 'Every part of the country has its own speciality.'

By his look he was using double meanings again, Marlie knew. She rose to the bait, wondering if this time she could hold her own. She had been lucky so far.

'I guess connoisseurs are always on the watch for the speciality,' she murmured. She had put just enough slur on the words for him to get her meaning.

His lips twitched slightly. 'How not? And tell me, who else but a connoisseur would know a speciality when he finds one?'

'I see your point,' Marlie smiled up at him. 'And it takes genuine experience to gain that knowledge—or instinct.'

'Knowledge, by all means. Most instincts are inborn.

Let's not make all that experience useless by calling it unnecessary. That's what makes finding that speciality, as we were calling it, so gratifying.'

Marlie was busy for a moment working that out. Since there seemed nothing to add, she tried a different tack.

'True enough, but tell me. If this—speciality—is capable of appreciating the compliment it's being paid, does it ever wonder if it is the ultimate discovery, or just another experience in the search for perfection?'

'Wouldn't that depend upon how it viewed itself?'

Marlie shook her head. 'Not at all, but how it was viewed. Nothing gives itself its true value, because nothing views itself objectively in relationship to its similarities.' Answering that should tangle his tongue, she thought smugly. But her smarting off could put her on dangerous ground too.

Greg's lips pursed thoughtfully. 'In that case the object, the—the—' His mouth pursued as he frowned down at her. 'Wait a minute! This conversation took a wrong turn somewhere!'

She threw back her head and laughed. Suddenly the night had increased in beauty as Greg laughed along with her. When he reached out, taking her hand, it was a natural reaction to wrap her fingers around his. They walked for some time, enjoying the night sounds of nature. Then the road began to rise and they climbed with it.

At the top of the low hill, by the edge of the road, the ground fell away sharply in the direction of the waterway. No trees blocked their view. Below them the channel stretched in a gleaming silver path, made all the more impressive by the surrounding darkness of the woods and marshes. They were barely sixty feet above the water level, but the land in the tidewater area was normally so flat that the little rise afforded a view that stretched for miles. Behind them a pine wood added a tangy odour to the evening air.

'A perfect place to put a house,' Greg said.

'Oh no!' Marlie cried. 'I would hate it if someone built up here. I like to think of it just as it is. I used to come here when I was a kid and this was my Everest, my Pikes Peak. It was the top of the world.'

Greg smiled down at her. 'Then you've been around here all your life?'

She nodded. 'Everybody has to grow up somewhere, and this is it for me.'

'Your parents?'

'My father works for the State Department. Right now he's with the Ambassador's staff in Italy. Mother is with him, of course.'

'Then you're not a poor little orphan?'

Marlie looked up, her expression blank. 'Did you think I was? I'm most certainly not an orphan, and I don't consider myself poor, though looking from your pinnacle of wealth I might be considered destitute.'

'Hey, peace.' Greg laughed. 'That was an expression—' He caught her by the shoulders and turned her around, gazing down on her face. His face held a serious expression. 'Did I come on as a snob? That's one accusation I'm not familiar with.'

'No, you didn't.' Marlie had to admit the truth. 'From anyone else I would have ignored it.'

'In other words, what's-his-name, who Doris mistook me for, could have gotten away with it.'

Marlie blinked. So that was still bothering him. 'If you mean we come from the same general background, the answer is yes.'

Greg's hands, still on her shoulders, gripped with more force. The firm line of his jaw seemed to become more prominent, the dark eyes, shadowed in the moonlight, were unreadable, but he seemed to loom larger, more threatening in Marlie's life. Without knowing why, she tried to step back, to fight against being drawn into the strength of this man who was enveloping her, though only his hands were on her shoulders.

'And that makes such a difference?' His face was drawing nearer to hers.

Hold on to your common sense, she reminded herself. Could the rest of her hear over the blood pounding in her ears she wondered?

'The similarities of background, of purpose in life—' Marlie's reasoning was inane, too often repeated, like a cliché, but with him so close she couldn't think.

'And that matters more than this?' His head bent, and his lips closed on hers. The desires he had aroused in her the night before were coming to the surface, flooding, eroding her thought, her strength. Some arbitrary part of her mind was still fighting him, the rest was yearning for the consuming fires.

His hands left her shoulders. One encircled her, drawing her softness against the bulwark of his chest. The other, cradling the flesh of her hip, lifted her nearly off her feet pressing her legs against his. She struggled and succumbed to the muscular strength that held her imprisoned.

Her mind was whirling in a dazed confusion of alarm and desire. A kaleidoscope of fears and hungers wove themselves into a pattern of frustration, fast being overridden by the waves of passion that rolled through her. With one hand she was struggling, with the other she was clinging when he raised his mouth from hers. He stepped back slight, and his hands moved back to her shoulders, unwilling to release her. His breathing was slightly ragged as he looked into her eyes.

'And tell me. What background does that show?'

'The connoisseur.' The words came out of their own volition, based on the recent conversation and his ability to entirely sweep her emotions. She hadn't considered the effect it would have on him. His mouth tightened in anger. She could feel the pain in her shoulders as his grip tightened.

'Would you say the connoisseur is still in search for perfection, or has he found it?'

Marlie was half afraid of the intensity in his voice, his expression, in his grip, but that spark of independence that was within her would not be denied.

'As I said before, the speciality would always wonder, wouldn't it?'

With his intake of breath, he seemed to grow before her eyes. More than half afraid, Marlie tugged at his hold on her shoulders. Her fingers weak and useless against his, plucked at his grip. He allowed her movement but kept pace with her. In the moonlight, as she backed across the road, she saw the gleam in his eyes, the ruthless determination that had made him a power in the financial world, and was trapping her.

Her feet felt the softness of pine needles under the soles of her shoes. She looked wildly around him, seeing he had allowed her to back from the tenuous safety of the road to the depths of shadows beneath the pines. She tried to turn, but he forced her to continue for an additional two steps.

She halted, her back against the roughness of pine bark. Reaching behind her, she felt a huge pine, one of the grandfathers of the wood. Greg was inexorably drawing closer.

Her eyes wide, helpless to prevent him, she watched his face. His determination blurred into hunger. She watched the slight flutter of his thick lashes and the parting of his lips, just before they met hers.

Softly, almost hesitantly, his tongue trailed across the delicate skin, exploring, drawing back, waiting for her reaction. The fear, the refusal that would have fought his force, crumbled under the gentle treatment. Some slumbering creature within her awakened, shook itself, and pushed forward. Lulled by the lack of threat, it reached out, hungering after its long hibernation.

His hands, so gentle and feather-light, left her shoulders and moved down her arms. They travelled with agonising slowness, exploring her skin beneath the thinness of the silk shirt. Feather-light, his fingertips circled and encircled her upper arms, leaving her skin tingling with a new and wondrous sensitivity. She felt with amazement the sensuality within herself which had remained hidden until Greg had awakened it.

Behind her the tree, in front of her she could feel the masculinity of his wide chest, the light press of his muscular thighs against hers. She was trapped, not by his arms, his grip upon her, but by the strength of her desire, the longing that moved through her body in hot waves.

His hands, still exploring, moved down to her forearms, teasing the tender skin, bringing an ache to her muscles. Emptiness created pain. Her arms needed to be pressed against him, holding him, giving in return, but when she tried to raise them she met resistance. He kept them by her side, denying her that simple release of longing. When she ceased to struggle, his hands travelled down to hers, caressing her fingers, awakening them to the exquisite pleasures of a caress. She wanted to cry out her pleasure, her distress, but his lips, still exploring hers, blocked her efforts.

His release of her hands was like a reprieve from some heinous but glorious prison. Her arms encircled him, her fingers caressed the short hair at the back of his neck, pulling his head closer, demanding more of his kiss than an elusive exploration that pulled away, leaving her hungering for more.

She longed for his arms to encircle her, to pull her close as he had on the yacht, but while she was denied that forceful pleasure, she found another in store. His hands moved to her sides, gently touching, raising goose bumps of desire around the swell of her hips. As slowly, as thoroughly as he had awakened the sensuality of the skin on her arms, her body became alive under his gentle exploring touch.

Without recognising her own voice, Marlie gave a little moan. She was pressed against him, revelling in his strong hard body, the masculine scent, pulling him tighter and tighter against herself.

Fully awakened to what would satisfy her hunger, she was, in retrospect, a little surprised that she had fought so hard against Greg. Only a foolish and blind woman would not recognise her need and its source. What if he had known other women before? Did she expect his life to be cloistered until he met her?

Desiring more of him, she moved his hand that was still torturing her side until it was cupped around her breast, but before her arm had encircled him again, he had dropped his hand, lightly fingering the outside of her thigh, still keeping his touch so light that one moment he was igniting fires, the next she wasn't sure he was there at all.

Desperately, she pulled him closer. Was he never going to stop his teasing? Her urgency had grown beyond her patience. She wanted him, was he never going to realise that? Was he going to forever play the game as if he were only interested in tuning an instrument—holding a glass of fine wine only to enjoy the bouquet? The thought came unbidden, but like a lightning bolt. Like a connoisseur? The idea was a cold shock. Her very being drew away like warm flesh from an icy hand.

With a rage fed by frustration, she shoved away from the tree, flinging herself out of his arms. She dashed several steps away before she turned to face him, her blush hidden by the shadows under the trees, her eyes blazing.

'You—you!' she shouted.

If she had expected him to be caught off guard surprised enough to lose the Alston cool, she was disappointed. Instead of dashing after her, he leaned against the tree, his arms folded across his chest.

'You—you connoisseur, you searcher for—for—'

'The specialities of life?' he suggested.

'Thank you,' she retorted. 'Trust you not to lose sight of your objective.' She turned towards the road, marching through the trees, and nearly fell over a large fallen branch. Before she could right herself she felt his hand on her arm, steadying her. 'Thank you, I can manage.'

'But surely you don't imagine such an experienced man with the ladies would leave one stumbling through the wood alone?'

His tone, so urbane, so filled with subtle humour, made her even angrier.

'Experienced is right!' she snapped as they came out on

the road. 'You must have to keep a file cabinet on your search for perfection. I'm not sure even then how you manage to keep them straight. I mean, with one female on deck while you're kissing another in the stateroom.'

There was the slightest pause before he smiled. 'Nice little girls don't say such things.'

'Nice little boys don't keep harems,' she retorted. 'And get one thing straight, Mr Alston. This—speciality—is one of a kind. And that apparently isn't your type, so just forget you ever met me.'

Marlie stumbled as her foot came down in one of the dry ruts that ridged the dirt road. He reached out and caught her arm, preventing her from falling.

'Forgetting you is going to be difficult if you keep trying to fall in a hole.' His composure was insulting.

'Thank you, but I did learn to walk at the normal age, and have managed for years,' she snapped.

All her resentments, and their reasons, came pouring back at once, including their first argument. 'And another thing.' Her blue eyes flashed as she stumbled and caught her balance. 'I don't need your advice on painting ducks!'

CHAPTER SIX

LOOKING back on Saturday night, Marlie was ashamed of herself. That was a hard, cold fact that coloured the next two days, but the true reason behind it was hiding in the chaos of her conflicting emotions. One by one she ticked off the possible reasons, filing them away again for future consideration.

Part of her problem was her loss of temper. She was a rational human being, not given to childish tantrums. How could she lose her control, act so immature? How did the man bring out that hidden part of her nature? Still, that wasn't all she had discovered about herself when she was with him. The awakening of a flaming desire that no other man had even stirred left her shaken and wondering at herself.

By Tuesday morning her mood had begun to lighten. After all, she would probably never see Greg again, so what was the point in staying angry? Thinking he might be hundreds of miles away, never planning on returning to Virginia Beach, left her as depressed as she had been irritated.

Her thoughts were interrupted as Howard approached her worktable.

'There's a delivery for you up in the front office,' he said. His casualness was elaborate, forced.

'What—I haven't ordered anything.' Then it occurred to her that her mother might have sent her something from Italy, not an uncommon happening. 'Just sign for it. I'll take a look when I've washed my hands.'

'Can't do it,' Howard replied. He was rocking back on his heels, his eyes focusing somewhere above her head. 'Man says he's instructed to leave it with you personally.'

'Of all the stupid—' Marlie rose from her stool, using a turpentine-soaked rag to wipe the paint off her hands. 'I hate to touch anything in this state, but let's see what's there.'

She entered the office to find a man in a delivery uniform holding a clipboard on which a pen was tied with a piece of cord.

'You Miss Marlie Richmond?' he asked.

'That's right.'

'If you'll just sign here, please, accepting delivery of that crate, the one sitting on the end of the truck, I'll bring it in.'

Marlie glanced through the dusty window, but she could only see an inch of what appeared to be a wooden crate. She took the pen and signed, handing the board back to the delivery man. The delivery would not be a present from her mother.

'Maybe someone sent me some oranges from Florida,' she said to Howard, who had walked into the office. Suddenly she was wary. Why had Fred, Norm and Paul followed Howard? Her eyes narrowed.

'What's going on?' she demanded. 'Are you pulling a practical joke?'

Howard raised his right hand solemnly. 'On our collective honour, we are not.' Was there the slightest emphasis on we?

Howard stepped over and opened the door as the delivery man came back, pushing a dolly. Marlie knew immediately that her first guess was wrong. Fruit came in smaller amounts. The crate was at least two feet high, with a length and width of approximately forty inches. Cardboard with evenly spaced holes an inch in diameter had been stapled to a wooden frame. She knelt by the box as the driver eased it off the dolly and made a hurried retreat. Through the holes she caught the silvery glint of wire. The unexpectedness of seeing a black eye appear at one of the holes made her draw back until she noticed the luminous green that surround it.

'There's a mallard duck in there,' she squealed, pulling away part of the cardboard.

Inside, she saw not one duck, but four. Closest to the wire screen was the mallard drake. His bright, metallic-green head was tilted, returning her inspection look for look. Behind him were two females, both drab in comparison. One was obviously his mate, and the other a female canvas-back. Her partner was standing in the opposite corner. His red-and-brown head was turned away, as if he disdained to honour the interruption with his attention.

'They're beautiful!' She waved Howard over. 'Look, aren't they gorgeous?'

'Sure are,' Paul answered, joining Marlie as she inspected the birds. 'Get a load of those mallards! Hey, that's some present.'

Marlie's eyes were wide as she looked at him. 'Who on earth would send me ducks? What am I going to do with them? Aren't they beautiful?' In her excitement her voice had risen, and she could hear it reverberating back at her from the walls. She lowered her voice. 'But where did they come from?'

'Maybe that will tell you,' Howard said, pointing to an envelope attached to the top of the crate.

Marlie grabbed and opened it, pulling out the single sheet of note paper. It read:

Dear Miss Richmond,

Thank you for a most enlightening visit to your factory.

I am sending you these four ducks, hoping you will benefit from having live models available.

Sincerely,

'Greg Alston!' Marlie wailed. 'That insufferable snob, that overtailored stuffed-shirt creep thinks I need models!' She jumped to her feet.

Howard retreated behind his desk. Fred slipped out of the office, followed by Norm and Paul, the latter unfortunate enough to let his smothered laugh be heard.

'Paul, you come back here!' Marlie shouted after him.

'Knew that boy was no fool,' Howard said as the doorway to the office remained empty.

'Fine,' Marlie stood with her arms akimbo. 'If you approve of his staying hidden, then you take care of these monsters.'

'Oh, no.' Howard leaned back in his chair, grinning. 'They're not my ducks, and I didn't hire Paul to look after livestock. Just wood-stock.' Howard chuckled over his own pun. 'And since when did they become monsters?'

'Well, they're not—' Marlie grudgingly conceded. 'But what am I supposed to do with them? The closest I've ever been to a real duck is at the meat counter in the supermarket.'

'Can't help that. You signed for them, you accepted them, they're your ducks.'

'But I thought they were oranges,' she insisted.

Howard leaned towards the crate. His eyebrows drew together, his mouth pursed thoughtfully. Marlie waited, hoping he had a solution. He slowly shook his head.

'No, don't think they're oranges.'

'That's just what I need—another jokester,' Marlie said with asperity. 'I want you to help me!'

'Okay, I'll help you.' He stood up and walked around the desk. 'Once again I will explain, they're not oranges, and they don't belong in my office. Now you get that end of the crate, I'll get the other. We'll take them back to your corner—one more word out of you, and you can manage by yourself.'

'Men,' Marlie said, after the crate had been lowered to the floor by her worktable. 'You're all alike, you all stick together. She glowered at Howard, who was squatting by the pen. 'Next, you'll be telling me I don't know how to paint—hey, that's my sandwich you're feeding that duck!'

'I thought you wanted my help,' Howard said, standing up. Marlie could see he was hiding his grin. 'I guess I'll mosey back to the office. Happy farming.'

Marlie sat on her stool, watching him go. His enjoyment of her discomfort was adding fuel to her indignation. It was just like him to think his precious fishing buddy could do no wrong, she thought.

When he was out of sight, she frowned down at the cage. What did Greg Alston think he was doing? She told herself that was silly. He knew what he was doing. Deadly insults were seldom handed out by accident. No one stumbled and dropped four live ducks by delivery van.

'You'll just sit right there until he comes and gets you,' she growled. She knew better. Welcome or not, they were alive, they had to have water, they had to be fed. Did they have to have exercise? She shook her head at the thought of walking ducks through the business district.

But in the interim, something had to be done for the birds. The weather man was predicting rising temperatures. The cardboard that had been fastened over the wire cage had probably protected the birds on their journey, but it cut off the ventilation. She knelt on the floor and tried tearing it away with her hands. After her second effort she sat back on her feet and decided another method would do the job with less wear and tear on her nails. From the painting table she took the screwdriver she used for prying off paint-can lids and worked it under the board where it had been tacked to the wood. Some minutes later she sat back, surveying Greg's gift. The sturdy wooden frame was covered by a meshed wire, and inside, ducks tilted their heads, inspecting her in turn.

'My, you are beauties,' she said.

Her voice broke the spell. The bright, metallic-green head of the mallard drake turned slowly, looking over the surroundings. His squawk was loud with more than a hint of disdain. The female mallard stepped towards Marlie and gave less raucous opinion.

Seeing the difference in the two birds of the same species, Marlie could feel a parallel between the birds and her problems with Greg Alston. Even the appearance coincided. The male mallard with his green head, the white band around his neck like a white collar, and the perfect rows of blue and white on his wings, looked as if he might have patronised Greg's tailor.

The female, patterned by nature to be camouflaged on the nest, was drab in comparison. The irregular design of her muted colouring gave a ragged, unkempt look. Marlie readily identified with the hen after her experiences with the king of the haberdasheries. She felt an immediate bond between herself and the female mallard.

'They do it to us every time,' she muttered. 'I bet that guy you fly around with is a feathered beast.' Marlie chose to accept the answering quack as an affirmative.

Further back in the cage a pair of canvas-backs were watching. They stood feather to feather, and any curiosity was satisfied from a distance. Marlie took exception to the complacency of the buff-and-grey female who was also paled by the presence of her more comely mate, but seemed not to resent it. Her drake was not as brilliant in his colouring as the mallard, but the dark brown on his beak, breast and top of his head was a strong contrast to the red on the back of his neck and under his eyes.

'I'll bet you catch his dinner,' she accused. Then she remembered that species ate only plants. She had forgotten what.

In the corner of the cage was a large, moulded, plastic dog dish. The two cuplike bowls were empty. One still showed moisture in the bottom.

'Not much hospitality on the delivery truck, I see,' Marlie said as she unfastened and raised the hinged top. She slowly inserted her hand and arm, poised to jerk back if one of the birds took exception, but while they quickened their interest, they made no offensive moves. Nor did they draw back out of reach.

When she stood up, she looked in the side of the empty container that had held food and wondered what in her lunch would appeal to them. While she thought it over she took the dish to the bathroom and washed it out, filling the water bowl. Back at the end of the paint table she looked at what was left of her sandwich and sighed. It wasn't much for four ducks, she thought, but it would stave off starvation until she could locate something more appropriate.

'Here you are.' She walked around the table to the cage and stopped. The wire enclosure was empty. 'What happened to the ducks?' she cried.

She whirled around in time to see Fred at the Howler. He was reaching for the switch to start the machine. Like a vehicle travelling too fast to turn suddenly, his hand, out of habit and its own momentum, hit the button. His expression turned from puzzlement to horror as the implications connected in his mind. The Howler roared to life only to be shut off immediately.

But the one roar had been enough to locate the birds. Quacking their fear, all four took wing. Like a covey of grouse rising from a bush, all four rose at once.

'Ya-hoo!' Paul shouted, his empty hands pantomiming a hunter sighting a quarry down the barrel of a gun.

'Stop that!' Marlie shouted, running around the end of a worktable. 'Help me catch them—umph!' Her eyes on the birds, she ran into Norm who was also watching their flight.

'They sure fly weird,' he said, dodging the female mallard who dived straight at him.

Marlie paused, looked up, and realised Norm was right. Not one bird could keep a straight course, nor did any fly well. Both drakes and the mallard female had crippled right wings. The canvas-back female had been injured on the left side. She was the strongest flyer. Unable to keep aloft for long periods, they were rising, making short curious flights and landing on whatever happened to be handy.

'We've got to catch them,' Marlie cried, afraid they would be hurt in a collision with the machinery. She started after the brightly coloured mallard drake. He was the most erratic. After getting a running start along a table he was airborne, swooping in circles.

Fred, who had been watching open-mouthed, made a leap towards the bird and fell over a tall stool sitting by the belt sander. While he was spreadeagled on the floor, the canvas-back, who was just landing, planted his feet firmly on Fred's hips. He ran up the machine operator's back as Fred was trying to rise and took wing again.

'They don't need any assistance,' Marlie called to Fred as she jumped over his legs, still chasing the mallard.

'If I wanted to be a runway, I'd join the airforce,' Fred griped as he jumped to his feet and kicked the stool under the table.

Howard, just coming out of his office, let out a yelp as the female canvas-back appeared to be aiming for his face. His fistful of invoices went flying as both hands went up to protect himself. Almost without intention he clasped the feathered body. The female voiced her protest and continued to flap her wings.

'Hold on to her!' Marlie called to Howard as she scrambled on to the table, still trying for the mallard. He was circling just out of her reach. As she made a grab for him, he dipped, sailing under her arm. With the added momentum, he changed his course. Determined to catch him, Marlie ran to the end of the sturdy table, jumping from it on to the one on which she painted. As she landed her foot slipped, causing her to fight for her balance. In the process her foot struck the can of green paint, sending it skittering along her work area before it overturned.

'Oh-h-h,' Marlie sighed. Howard had rapidly crossed the room with the canvas-back female and was bent over the cage at the end of the table. Green paint dripped from his arm and down his trouser leg. Fortunately, he and the floor had taken most of the splash, but there were several drops of paint on the duck.

Across the room, Paul was stumbling across the top of a bin heaped with the three-foot lengths of wood that had been cut for carving. As the female mallard winged about erratically, lit and flew again, Paul tripped and staggered about, knocking wood from the bin.

'Hey, watch it!' Norm yelled as he chased the male canvas-back that had given up the air in favour of running between the bins and under the equipment tables.

Marlie shook her head as the chaos increased. A yelp from Fred caused her to turn. He was scrambling up from the floor again, swearing at the duck he chased and Paul, who had knocked the wood on the floor. Not content with them, he had a few choice words about the company for giving him a job, and the President, who should have passed a law against everything.

A swish of wings by her shoulder startled Marlie and she jumped back. The mallard drake made an awkward landing on the shelf where she kept the drying ducks. He turned an inspecting eye on his wooden counterparts. Then, stretching his neck, he nibbled at the sleeve of Marlie's blouse.

'Why, you faker! You're not wild at all!' The indignation that should have sent him flying again, earned her a loud, oblique reply. With the rapid thrust of his neck and bill, he caught the end of the red ribbon, tied above Marlie's ear, and gave a tug.

'Behave yourself!' she said, picking him up. 'You stay right here on the table until I get down—watch out, you're walking in that spilled paint!' Marlie scrambled down from the table, a task made more difficult by trying to keep the bird out of the cans that were still upright. By now

Howard had closed the top of the cage, so Marlie stood the drake on the floor, and considering the perversity of the males in her life, wasn't surprised that he took the opportunity to step into the paint on the ground before him. His webbed feet left perfect tracks as he walked over to the stool. When he was out of reach, Marlie decided to forgo chasing him. There was an easier way to catch a tame duck. She picked up the dish of food and water, tapping on the side until he turned to identify the noise. He gave a loud quack and came, on the run.

His call for food alerted his mate and the male canvasback. The red-headed male charged out from between two cartons, evaded Fred, and he, too, ran through the spilled paint. He was trying to climb into the wire enclosure before Marlie could put the mallard in and give him a lift. The mallard female made the trip almost as quickly, taking long fluttering jumps.

'Why didn't you try that in the beginning?' Howard demanded.

'You needed your exercise,' Marlie retorted. She glanced around the room at the havoc and sat down on her stool, her chin in her hand. 'This isn't happening,' she told Howard. 'It's all a bad dream.'

'Such is real life sometimes,' Howard grinned suddenly. The paint on his arms and clothes seemed to be forgotten.

Marlie straightened and shook her head. 'Reality can't be like this, it has to be a—what are you laughing at?' She needed no answer. Her right hand, the one that had been holding her chin, was streaked with green. It came from her handling the mallard duck who had struggled in his desire to get to the food in the cage.

'He's done it to me again!' she wailed. 'Greg Alston's not even here and he did it—' She started for the ladies' room, then turned back to Howard, her eyes flashing, her fists clenched in frustration. 'And if you tell him, I'll—I—I'll never paint another duck as long as I live!' Near to tears, she ran towards the front of the building, nearly tripping over Paul as he picked up the wood in the centre aisle.

Five minutes later, her face clean, her hair combed, and her shirt tucked neatly in her jeans, she marched back out to the production area.

In her absence, the cage had been lifted and placed on the packing table. Fred was busy with a hammer and some small nails.

'You pulled the wire loose when you took off the cardboard,' he said, explaining how the ducks had escaped. Marlie stood gazing at the birds. They appeared none the worse for their escape and the chase. She wondered just how frightened they had been. Fred's hammering on the side of the cage seemed to be of intense interest to them. The canvas-back hen was happy enough. The others were moving hesitantly, picking up their legs and shaking them because of the paint that coated the bottoms of their feet and the webbing between their toes.

Marlie wondered how to remove it. Did she dare use paint or varnish remover? She decided against it, not knowing how sensitive their skin might be. First she would try something more soothing. She lifted the wire top and took the mallard drake under her arm.

'I shouldn't bother with you at all,' she told him. 'You're the one that caused me to kick over the can.'

Back in the ladies' room again, she took a jar of cold cream from the personal items she kept in the small cabinet. She lowered the seat on the toilet and sat down, holding the bird in her lap.

'Now this might work if you co-operate,' she told the duck. With the cream on both hands she started smearing his webbed feet. Either he was ticklish, or he objected to sitting on his tailfeathers, because he squawked and kicked. 'Wait just a minute!' she protested, trying to hold his slippery feet with slippery fingers. 'Be still, will you?'

He ceased his struggles, but not because of her command. The jar of cold cream had arrested his attention. Before she could stop him he arched his neck and stuck his bill in the jar. With a disgusted hiss he shook his head and wiped his bill on her cheek.

'Oh, you pest!' Marlie grabbed a handful of tissues from a box and wiped her face, his bill, and started on his feet. The still wet paint had mixed with the cold cream and spread, in their struggle, from his webbed feet up his legs. He appeared to be wearing bright green boots.

'I've failed again,' she muttered as she took him back to the cage.

Norm and Fred, working together, had wiped most of the paint off the feet of the other ducks, but on all three, the stains would remain for some time.

'If Greg Alston sees that, I'll never live it down,' she muttered. There was no doubt in her mind that he would see them. She stood very still, her eyes narrowing. Then why not make it immediately, she thought. It meant hearing him laugh at her, but the ducks came from him, and he should be the one to take care of them. She certainly could not keep birds in her apartment nor at the factory. Maybe the yacht was still at the marina.

Paul had cleared the aisles and was preparing to clean up the spilled paint.

'Leave that for a minute,' Marlie told him. 'Get Norm, and the two of you bring the cage out to the station-wagon.' She wordlessly held out her hand to Howard, waiting for him to give her the keys.

He was reluctant. 'What are you planning? You can't drive to the nearest river and open the pen. They'd never survive.'

'No, but I can return a gift. Greg Alston can give them a stateroom or tow them behind his yacht—the choice is his.' Her harsh words caused her to pause, wondering if he would take proper care of them. She decided she was being unjust. He was not the type of man to be thoughtless of animals, she was sure. She held out her hand again and, with a sigh, Howard handed her the keys.

During the drive Marlie tried to rehearse her speech to Greg Alston.

'I thought it was a darling joke,' she experimented, checking her smile in the rear-view mirror.

A raucous noise interrupted from the wire pen. She glanced in the mirror again to see the birds looking in her direction.

'You're right. Maybe I should just kick him in the shins. That would be more in character, after the way I've behaved recently.'

The mallard drake gave her his opinion. His loud voice grated on Marlie's already tight nerves, not because of the volume, but his authoritative tone reminded her of the man she would soon be seeing.

'That's all you know about it. Just because you're a male, you're not guaranteed to be infallible, you know.'

The blare of horns brought Marlie back to reality. She slammed the brake pedal to the floor just in time to avoid a collision. She looked up at the light, which was a bright, glaring red. The following thunk caused her to think she had been struck by one of the cars that had also screamed to a stop. Then she realised the pen holding the ducks had slid forward. Startled by their collision with the cage and each other, they renewed their clamour.

Marlie waited until the light changed, feeling conspicuous as the wagon blocked the pedestrian walk and the cross traffic manoeuvred around her.

She felt like sinking in the seat as she watched the inconvenience she had caused. She was overcome by guilt because she should have been paying attention to her driving, not arguing with a duck. That admission left her slightly incredulous. The week before she had been a sensible schoolteacher on vacation. Five days of knowing Greg Alston had reduced her to blocking traffic and fighting with birds.

I should kick him in the shins, she thought. She savoured the idea as she drove to the marina.

Marlie wheeled into the sandy parking lot near the yacht and backed the station-wagon into a convenient position to unload the birds. The near accident as she came through town had erased from her mind all thought of trying to outwit Greg. She just wanted to deliver the ducks and escape without being embarrassed again.

She stepped out into the bright sunlight and closed the door on the vehicle, leaving the window down so that the birds could get the breeze. Henry was just leaving the boat with a suitcase. When he saw her he altered his direction to approach her.

'Miss Richmond,' he said in surprise. 'I'm sorry, but if you wanted to see Mr Alston, you are too late by a day. He will be in New York until Friday.'

'And you're joining him?' Marlie realised her question was prying, but she had been so disappointed at not finding Greg aboard, that she asked without thinking. But

Henry explained willingly.

'No, I'm on my way to Baltimore. My brother is in need of assistance for a few days and Mr Alston has given me time off until Friday afternoon.'

Marlie looked at the large, well-kept boat. 'Surely there is someone aboard,' she said. 'I like the ducks Mr Alston sent, but there's no way I can keep them. One of the crew can feed and water them until he returns.'

Henry's good humour dissolved into resignation. 'I don't think Mr Alston would approve of that. I'd better stay. Our crew is made up of first-class sailors, but I doubt Mr Alston would trust them to care for his ducks. He's very particular about them.'

'I don't think that's necessary,' Marlie retorted. 'If Greg Alston thought they were too delicate for a sailor to feed, he wouldn't have used them for a silly joke, shipping those poor things around, probably scaring them half to death. That is not my idea of a compassionate man.'

Henry bowed his head in an unsuccessful attempt to hide his laugh. He gave up trying to be discreet and chuckled out loud.

'I wouldn't want to see anything that would scare them. They think they own the farm in Maryland.' His plump form shook as he tried to stop laughing. Then his eyes turned serious.

'I don't think you know Mr Alston well enough to understand, Miss Richmond. I wasn't privy to the arrangements, but I know he would never trust those birds to strangers. Because they're crippled, he takes a keen interest in their welfare. I'm not sure what you mean by insult, but I can assure you he would not honour many people with that much confidence in their character. Mr Alston has a great man's aversion to mistreatment of the

helpless. I would say you've made quite an impression on
my employer.' Henry's smile was kind.

Marlie's blue eyes sparkled with frustration. She stuffed
her hands in the pockets of her jeans as she gazed at
Henry. She was momentarily at a loss for words and was
finding it difficult to give up her plans for revenge. Deep
down, she knew she had been enjoying them. Henry was
pulling away all her excuses for fighting with his boss.

'Greg Alston has a farm?' she asked, looking for a chink
in the impression Henry presented of his employer.

Henry nodded. 'He breeds race horses. We're close to
the marshes and occasionally an injured bird gets away
from a hunter or is caught in a storm and hurt. I suppose
we shelter at least thirty.'

Marlie caught the change in Henry's explanation that
bared his pride in Greg, and his involvement in his job.

'I'll take care of them until the weekend,' Marlie said
slowly. Half of her wanted to acknowledge the compliment Henry had suggested, but the other half was resist-
ing. On the drive out to the marina she had been frus-
trated by not having a plan to outwit Greg. Now she
would have more time. She threw a dark look at Henry.

'But he's not to know we had this talk.'

Henry's lips pursed; his eyes twinkled. 'Of course not.'

Before she left him, Henry had told her when he
expected to arrive back aboard the yacht, in the event she
needed to return the birds as early as possible to free her
weekend. The information that Greg was due just an hour
or so later than his employee, was, Marlie thought,
volunteered with an air of anticipation.

As she drove back to town, she was certain Henry was
looking forward to the weekend and its possible diver-
sions.

CHAPTER SEVEN

MARLIE's thoughts were in a tumble as she drove back to town. Because of her talk with Henry, she had an insight into Greg Alston that was new and disturbing. She had thought of him as unfeeling with his joke, and yet, according to the picture Henry had painted, Greg was trusting her not to take out her indignation on the helpless.

She wouldn't, of course. She hoped she was more fair-minded, but how did he know that? Obviously he had read that part of her character, but how, what had brought him to that point? What had she done? A good feeling invaded her. In spite of their bickering, she had won his good opinion.

Hold it, she warned herself. Remember, he's not just any man, but Greg Alston. She concentrated on what she knew about him. A man successful with women. He had another on the string that she knew about—a beautiful socialite—and probably more, yet he was trying to add her to his harem. A man that experienced with women would know the science of compliments. How he knew this particular one would work with her, she couldn't imagine.

Yes she could. He was using that connoisseur's experience. Her cheeks grew hot as she remembered Saturday evening. She had considered herself worldly-wise after more than her share of struggles with amorous males. She was wary of their passes, games and tricks, but those of Greg Alston were entirely new to her. She was embarrassed again as she remembered how she had succumbed to his advances.

'He should be outlawed,' she muttered.

The answer from the wire pen startled her. For a moment she had forgotten the ducks. Reminded, she gritted her teeth and tried to think of some appropriate reprisal for his latest insult, but her mind balked. Intruding into her thoughts with growing regularity came the pangs of hunger.

No wonder, she thought, looking down at her watch. She was accustomed to having her lunch at twelve-thirty, and two o'clock had passed. Her favourite restaurant was two blocks away, but she was in her painting clothes, and she could hardly leave the vehicle in the parking lot. The ducks could succumb to heat prostration in the closed car, and if she left the windows open, they might end the day on dinner platters.

Three blocks farther on, she spotted a fast-food restaurant that had a drive-through lane for take-out orders. When she pulled up at the sign that displayed the menu and held the intercom, she saw a note.

Speaker out of order.

As she drove up to the window, she slightly misjudged her stop. She was too far forward. By the time she adjusted the rear-view mirror so that she could see over the cage to back up, two cars had pulled in behind her. The confusion involved in requiring them to move back was more than she felt she could handle after her day of upsets. She was close enough to pay and receive her order, but she had to turn in her seat to speak to the fresh-faced youth at the window.

'A cheese burger and a coke, please.'

The birds had been quiet, but when she spoke the

mallard drake started to quack, accompanied by the two females. Marlie eyed them, wondering how to prevent their noise. Of course, they could be hungry again. If they were fed maybe they would sleep. She knew mallards in the wild fed on insects and grain, and that could be loosely translated into meat and bread. Twice she tried to speak, but she was forced to wait until the birds finished their harangue.

'And give me two regular hamburgers,' she said, gazing back at the boy. His brows knotted together as he looked from Marlie to the ducks and back again. The mallard male quieted, but his lady still had a few comments.

Marlie, getting frayed nerves from the racket turned slightly, and considered banging on the cage. She decided against it. If she frightened them the noise could continue indefinitely. She waited for them to pause before amending her last request.

'Make those last two burgers plain,' she said, not sure ducks liked mustard and pickles.

She wondered what was bothering the clerk. He stared from her to the birds and back as if he had never seen a duck. And his eyes were wary. Did he think they were going to get out of the cage?

The mallards had quieted, but the canvas-back started making himself known. His quacks were barely audible, and Marlie frowned. Was he hurt or sick? As she focused her attention on him, she remembered his normal diet was wild celery.

'And a salad, no dressing,' Marlie added. By now the kid was frowning, biting his lip. His eyes travelled in a circle, from the order to her and on to the ducks.

His attitude was puzzling. 'Is something wrong?' she asked. She knew better than to take an animal inside a restaurant, but surely there was no reason why they couldn't be in the car while she ordered. Possibly she was taking too much time, but while the birds were creating so much racket, she had trouble thinking or being heard.

He threw a furtive glance over his shoulder, then leaned forward, making sure his voice was inaudible to the others in the restaurant. He jerked a thumb in the direction of the cage.

'Did that one with the green head say anything about french fries?'

Marlie closed her eyes, trying to keep control of her temper. She had had as much of male superiority as she could stand. That kid was hardly old enough to shave, yet he was already trying to make a fool out of a woman. She was speechless for a moment. Turning, she looked into the cage. For once, the ducks were quiet. The male mallard, who could usually be counted upon to give out with a disdainful quack, was busy smoothing his feathers. When he looked up he sounded positively friendly.

She might have let Greg Alston get the upper hand, but no team of males made up of a duck and a smart-mouthed kid was going to get away with it. She looked the boy straight in the eye.

'He says "thank you, but he's on a diet." '

Once away from the restaurant, she pulled over in the shade of a tree. Two hamburgers were too much for the mallards, she decided, she tore one into duck-bite sized pieces and did the same with the salad before putting the food in the cage. She made a mental note to thereafter feed the ducks when she had her meals. Their table conversation left a lot to be desired, but they were reasonably quiet.

The birds were becoming accustomed to riding, and

they were sound asleep when she pulled into the parking lot at the factory.

'You brought them back?' Howard frowned when she wanted Paul and Norm to bring in the cage.

'Temporarily,' Marlie sighed and told him why she hadn't left them on the boat. 'I can't take them to my apartment. If we keep them here, we can't run the Howler, it's too loud—it scares them.'

'Then you're going out to the cabin?' Howard's question supplied the only answer, and they both knew it. He shrugged. 'Why not? You're caught up, and you should take some time off.'

'Great vacation, looking after a quartet of spoiled ducks.' Howard's sharp look brought out a desire to tell him about ordering lunch, but she bit back the impulse. He would tease her for years.

'I'll just leave them here while I do some laundry and pack. In this heat they'd be roasted in an hour if I left them in the car.'

Marlie was considerably more than an hour in her apartment. While the washer and dryer did their stuff, she searched her wardrobe. As she planned her packing, she removed several outfits from the closet, inspected, considered, and put them back. Many were too dressy to take to the cabin. The orange sundress was her favourite, but she had worn that when she had dinner on the yacht.

'I need new clothes,' she informed her reflection in the mirror. The blue eyes that gazed back at her were teasing, questioning, as if they heard something in that remark she had not considered. Well, why not, a part of her muttered. She deserved something new and she remembered reading that women won half their battles with the masculine sex by the appearance they made. She wasn't going to upgrade her wardrobe because of Greg Alston, however. What she bought, she would get because she needed it.

Sure, came a little voice from inside, but she firmly shut it away.

She refused to let doubts enter her head. The additional time she spent in the department store before she returned to the factory was, in her mind, well spent. She wasn't so sure about her depleted bank account.

But the new outfits were carefully tucked away when she arrived at the cabin. Greg would be out of town for the next three days, and she needed to turn her mind to her reprisal. The next move was hers, and she was determined to make it a good one.

Tuesday evening and Wednesday morning were lost because no brain would function over the racket of the ducks. Not until she threatened to drown the entire quartet did she realise their problem. They could see the water from their cage and were demanding a swim.

She felt guilty for keeping them penned up, but did she dare just turn them loose? She thought not. Perhaps a leash. On a duck? A strong cord knotted around the leather-like ankle would do, she decided. Ten noisy minutes later, she held four cords as the birds ran for the water. She frowned at the four men in a small boat who laughed as they passed.

The rest of the morning was peaceful. While the birds paddled about on their long leads, Marlie considered her problem. Greg could not be allowed to get away with his little joke. If she was to believe Henry, it was not the insult she had at first believed, but retaliation was necessary to her self-respect.

It still bothered her that he had been so trusting with the birds. Suppose he had been wrong in his judgment of her. She could have been the type to chop the heads off the poor creatures without a second thought. It would serve him right if she had. Of course, the ducks might have some objection, but Greg Alston needed to be taught a good lesson.

A glimmer of an idea lit the back of her mind, and was just shimmering into brilliance when Doris strolled around the side of the cabin. She raised her hand in greeting, but stopped with her mouth open as she saw the ducks and the confining cords that were tied to the nearest tree.

'Just the person I need,' Marlie called, jumping up from her chair. 'You've just been elected to entertain my guests while I make a dash for the store.' She left while Doris was still too stunned to object.

After her shopping, Marlie settled down to a peaceful afternoon. The birds were happy, and she spent the rest of the day, as well as all of Thursday, enjoying the river, planning her revenge, and chasing away a shivery tingle as her thoughts kept returning to Greg Alston.

Friday morning she awakened with the knowledge that Greg was due back that evening. She thought back on her conversation with Henry, who was planning to arrive at the boat just an hour before Greg. Marlie knew her plan would require perfect timing. She wanted to see and talk to Henry, but if Greg demanded a confrontation, he would have to drive out to the cabin. She had no doubt he would. He would be unable to resist, if her plan worked. If it didn't . . . she shuddered.

The morning passed quickly as she spent her time between cleaning the cabin and watching the ducks as they swam. At two o'clock she turned on the oven and removed the defrosted fowl from the refrigerator. She diced oranges, grated the peel and busied herself with the stuffing while the oven heated. Finished with that, she made her preparations for hers and Howard's dinner, knowing they might be having a guest.

She checked the clock as she straightened the kitchen and slid the fowl in the oven. Pleased with her arrangements she strolled into the bathroom for a leisurely soak. She gave particular attention to her hair, curling it so it fell in soft waves. Her manicure was time-consuming, but perfect. The new blue trouser-suit was darker than her eyes, giving them additional colour. She carefully applied her make-up, liking the new shade of lipstick. Her summer tan had given her a need for a slightly darker shade. Her new sandals were perfect with her outfit. When she was dressed, she approved of what she saw in the mirror. She had made her plans carefully; she should not see Greg, but it was wise to be prepared. If he had changed his schedule and she confronted him on the boat, it would be to her advantage to look her best.

Back in the kitchen, she wrapped a large apron around her new outfit and removed the cooked duck from the oven. If the taste matched the appearance, she would have nothing to be ashamed of. She slid it on to the platter and covered it with foil. With a piece of scotch tape, she attached the note she had written that morning. If Henry was keeping to his schedule, he should arrive at the boat no more than ten minutes before her. He would not have had time to prepare dinner for his boss.

Marlie had timed her plans even closer than she had expected. When she brought the car to a halt in the parking lot, Henry was just crossing the deck, suitcase in hand. By the time she stepped aboard he was out of sight. An elderly crewman who appeared from the port side, took her message to Greg's personal servant while she waited in the lounge.

Henry was all smiles when he entered. 'Miss Richmond, did you bring the ducks?'

'Well, I brought a duck,' she replied, allowing him to read the attached note. In her best copperplate she had written: The others were delicious.

She felt guilty when he paled. Since he must have known she was planning her revenge, she had not expected a reaction from him.

'Now, Henry, how could I know they were pets?' she paused and gave him a broad wink. 'We did not have our little talk, remember?'

His breath expelled in a deep sigh as he grinned. 'You gave me quite a scare, Miss Richmond.'

Marlie laughed. 'I just wish you could have seen your face. If you could serve it with that expression, I would be grateful.'

Henry shook his head emphatically. 'It's impossible—I could never serve it—not if you want Mr Alston to believe it—' he hesitated, seeing her dismay. 'The far more effective route would be for me to show it to him with an attitude of outrage. He knows I would never put one of his pets before him on a platter.'

'Of course not,' Marlie cried, her eyes wide. 'Why didn't I think of that?' For a moment she was stunned by her lack of foresight. Then she nodded thoughtfully. 'Still, showing it to him as you suggested will do as well.'

Marlie left hurriedly, since as much as she would like to see Greg's face, she did not want to be on the boat when he arrived. Battles were always easier on one's home ground, she had heard, and if his wrath brought him out to the cabin as she expected, she could stop his anger at any time by simply showing him his pets were safe and sound.

When she arrived back at the cabin, the ducks were indeed safe and sound, but angry at her for leaving. Not that she blamed them. The afternoon was hot, even in the shade, and they wanted a swim. She hurried into the kitchen to start dinner and returned with a large apron to protect her clothing while she tied the cords to their legs. As she worked, she sighed. No matter what she did, nothing would prevent Greg from seeing the paint on the ducks' feet. She could imagine the remarks, and just thinking about them caused her to flinch. She finished tying a cord to the foot of the canvas-back drake and stood him on her lap, shaking her finger at his bill.

'I warn you—if you love your master, when he comes around, squat, because if he makes one remark about your feet, I'll—I'll kick him in the shins!'

As she followed them to the bank, trotting because of their haste, she was determined that nothing was going to ruin her carefully made up appearance before she saw Greg again.

The ducks weren't in the water more than five minutes before she realised she had made a mistake. Friday afternoons the traffic on the waterway was heavy. The centre of the channel was periodically being used by large pleasure boats and the smaller, faster craft were zipping in close to the bank. Over their objections, she brought the ducks back to shore, towing them in by the cord attached to their feet.

While they complained at the interruption of their swim, she untied the boats moored in the slip and pushed them further out into the stream. No one would run into them, but few of the fishermen would pay attention to birds, thinking they could fly out of danger. After the trick she had pulled on Greg, if anything happened to one of his pets, she would never convince him she hadn't been careless.

Once in the water again, the ducks quieted. They had a new area to explore, and Marlie sat back, watching the river traffic. She was keeping a close eye on her watch as well. If Greg kept to his schedule, the earliest he could arrive to confront her was half an hour away. She wanted the ducks quiet and out of sight until she chose to tell him they were in their cage. After their swim, if they were well fed, they might settle down and doze, she decided. She filled their dishes and one by one, she towed them in, untied their cord leashes, and put them in the cage. She had three in the pen when she went back to the slip to get the mallard drake. His cord was still tied to the mooring post, but he was not at the other end.

'Oh, no!' she cried and ran around the boats. No duck. She looked up and down the waterway, half expecting to see him paddling out in front of a speedboat. She was only partly relieved by not seeing him in danger. Her big worry was that she didn't see him at all.

'You—male!' she muttered. 'When I find you, you may end up in the oven after all.'

She walked around the slip, checking to see if the drake had hidden himself between the boats or between them and the wooden sides of the slip. She even checked the yard, thinking he might have left the water to chase an insect, but no duck.

He had to be on the water, she decided. She untied the rope and jumped down into her ten-foot boat, glad she had put the motor on it only that morning. One push of the pole and the small boat floated out into the river. She lost no time in starting the engine, intending to search up and down the river. But the roar of the motor flushed her quarry. With a spate of frightened quacking, the mallard came out from under an overhanging bush and half paddled, half flew into the safety of the slip.

Marlie pointed the boat back towards its berth and cut the motor after one jog of the throttle. She drifted after the bird, blocking his escape by water.

'Now, you stay right where you are,' Marlie told him. She tied up the boat and jumped ashore.

The mallard floated close to the end of the slip, but when she approached him, he swam slowly out of reach.

'Now you stop that!' she demanded and circled to the other side, but he drifted off as she approached. He was casual to the point of insolence, staying just beyond her, moving so slowly he could have been pushed by the breeze.

'You green-headed monster,' Marlie snarled through gritted teeth. 'It's easy to see you've learned from your master, but if you think you can get away from me, you think again!'

Tired of chasing him around the slip, she stepped into her boat and moved up into the bow. By use of the emergency oar, she moved the craft slowly forward. When she was within reach, she dropped the oar and leaned over the side. As her fingers touched the feathers on his back he spread his wings and tried to fly. Marlie made a grab for an outstretched wing and tumbled into the water.

She came up sputtering. While she was under the water, her head had contacted the wooden side of the slip, not hard enough to be considered a bump, she decided. As she stood, waist deep in the water, clouded by the muddy bottom, she put the fingers of her left hand to her forehead.

The darkened fingertips, as she inspected them, looking for blood, told their story. She was wearing the mud residue that had clung to the planking.

Ruined again, she thought. A strand of hair, stringy and dripping with muddy water, hung over her forehead and across her face. The new trousers and shirt were streaked with mud and plastered to her skin. She could feel the mud between her toes as her new sandals sank deeper into the soft bottom.

With no surprise, but with a sense of utter futility, she watched Greg Alston striding across the grass. A glance at her water-soaked watch showed he was on time to the minute.

'Wonder if I can drown myself,' she muttered. At that moment a watery death seemed preferable to facing him after her dunking. She held her nose and slipped under the surface, intending to make her way submerged to the shelter of the boats four feet away. She had hardly started when a strong hand grabbed her arm and pulled her upright. Still holding her nose, she looked up from under her wet brows.

He was glaring down at her, his face darkened with anger. His strong square jaw out-thrust, the cords of his neck standing out in tension above his white collar. That gleaming white collar! She hated that collar! What right had he to be so clean and shining? His perfection was suddenly past all bearing.

'How dare you eat those ducks?' he shouted at her.

'How dare you be so clean?' she shrilled. Without thought, with an instinct born of her frustration, she reached up, grabbed his arms, and planted her feet against the wooden side of the slip. Greg, half squatting, leaning over the water, was helpless against her sudden jerk. The surprise on his face as he sailed over her head, did wonders for Marlie's injured dignity.

Her heart sang when he stood up, his dark hair dripping muddy water, his white collar a mottled brown. He was still angry, but his shock at being pulled into the slip had taken precedence.

'You—you—' He tried a menacing step in her direction, but the muddy bottom was slippery and he nearly lost his balance. While Marlie faced him defiantly, out from behind the bow of her small boat swam the mallard drake. He silently moved up behind Greg and stretched his neck to nibble at his hand.

'Sick 'em,' Marlie ordered just as the duck's bill closed on Greg's little finger.

Thinking he had been attacked, Greg tried to jump away, lost his footing and went under again. Marlie had backed up to the edge of the slip and watched as he surfaced. He came up eye to eye with the mallard.

Even if he hadn't recognised the bird as his own, it was ready to take possession of him. After a casual glance at his face the mallard stretched his neck and tugged at a lock of Greg's hair. With a gentle but firm hand, Greg stroked and pushed the duck back away from his face as he stood, the water running down his shirt and arms.

'What are you doing, turning my own ducks against me?' he demanded.

'That one, at least,' Marlie retorted. She still wasn't ready to admit the others existed, but they had ideas of their own. They set up a clamour, and even though their pen was out of sight, there was no doubt about the source of the noise.

Greg looked at her blankly for a moment. His gaze dropped to the mallard who was busily trying to eat the large gold ring on his left hand. Marlie could see in his eyes his struggle to lay aside his anger, and knew the feeling. To build a rage on a premise that later proved to be false, required an emotional readjustment. But he was fast getting himself under control. His mouth, that had been tight, widened into an evil grin. His deep grey eyes gleamed as they narrowed.

'You devil,' he murmured and started in her direction. 'You are going to pay for that little trick!'

'You stay away from me!' Marlie cried. She grabbed the well-anchored mooring post and scrambled on to the grass. Her intention was to make a dash for the dubious safety of the cabin.

Greg scorned pursuing her across the slip. Instead he reached for a support on his side, and in one leap was on the grass and running. He was between Marlie and the cabin so, denied her refuge, she circled the flower bed, depending on his respect for the flowers to keep him on the border. Directly across from her he waited, giving her the right to make the next move.

The tailored perfection that had so irritated Marlie had been overcome by the muddy water. His hair streamed in his face unregarded. A smear of mud streaked down his cheek, another spotted his left arm, but he ignored them. Rather than detracting from his masculinity, his soaking clothes clung to his body, revealing his wide chest, his muscular arms and thighs. His dishevelled state accentuated that wild look Marlie had seen in the torchlight on the yacht. Like some magnificent savage, he was half crouched, balancing on the balls of his feet as he swayed back and forth, alert to every nuance of her movement.

The flicker of his eyes, as he took in her appearance, reminded her of her own state. The silk shirt was embarrassingly transparent, causing her to feel naked under his gaze. She desperately wanted to escape to her room and dry clothing, still his obvious appreciation gave her a thrill, reminding her of her own sensuality as well as his.

'You stay away from me,' she threatened again as she moved back and forth, seeking an escape. 'You deserved it!'

'And you deserve what you're going to get,' he answered, his smile turning satanic. With a sudden leap he cleared the flowers and jumped to the narrow cleared path between the plants and the stump that had been cut to resemble a chair.

Knowing she had to flee, and fast, Marlie turned and ran. Too late she realised she had trapped herself. Directly ahead was the river bank, barely two feet above the water level. As she tried to check her stride she was grabbed from behind, lifted and thrust forward. She could feel Greg's body against her as they splashed down into the water.

Although the middle of the channel was deep enough to carry ocean-going vessels, immediately adjacent to the bank a shelf less than two feet deep had been left by the dredging equipment.

Marlie and Greg floundered in a tangle of legs as they both sought to gain their balance. Marlie heard, but paid no attention to, the quacking of the mallard as he half ran, half flew across the yard in their direction.

'Oh, you asked for it!' Marlie sputtered. Grabbing a handful of bottom mud, she flung it at Greg, who wasn't quite fast enough to dodge. She missed his face, but did manage to splatter his neck and shoulder.

'You must feel absolutely naked,' Greg retorted. With his left hand he grabbed her shoulder, keeping her within reach. With his right, he smeared her cheek, then leaned back, surveying her appraisingly. His brows went up. 'Now I recognise you!'

'I hope so!' Marlie disdained to clean her face. Instead she flung another handful of the black bottom soil.

Greg, expecting it, successfully dodged. Marlie scored a direct hit on the mallard, who was preparing to join the swimming party. The bird gave an outraged squawk and staggered on the edge of the bank, shaking his head.

'You're taking it out on the duck?' Greg teased.

'Well, he started it,' Marlie muttered, sounding like one of her students. She was ashamed of having hit the poor thing, but it wouldn't do to let Greg know that.

They tactfully called a time out while Greg picked up the angry bird and dumped him in the water, head down. The bright green legs and webbed feet thrashed in the sunlight.

Just let him open his mouth, Marlie thought, her jaw tight, both hands full of mud.

He surprised her by not mentioning the paint, but while acting so concerned about the bird, he still managed to sling a handful of mud in her direction. Marlie was quick enough to turn her head, but felt the wet glob strike her hair.

'Never trust a man,' she cried, retaliating in kind.

The mud was flying fast and furious when a sardonic voice from the bank startled them both.

'Is this how the rich and famous play?' They looked up to see Howard, arms akimbo, looking down at them.

Marlie, with a handful of black goo, altered her swing without pause. She barely missed Howard, who made his retreat at a dead run. Greg came closer to the target, but Howard dodged just in time.

'Enough fun and games,' Greg said, climbing the bank. 'If you think you've worked off your childish energies—' He held out his hand to assist her, but she noticed his legs were braced. He was wary of her.

Marlie bit back a retort. That was exactly what he wanted.

'You're right, of course,' she lowered her eyes. 'I do let my enthusiasms run away with me.' She meekly held up her hand, accepting his assistance. Not until she was standing on the bank did she realise they had overlooked the reason she had first been dunked.

'We forgot the duck,' she objected.

Greg gave a whistle. 'Come on, Caesar.'

Obediently, the mallard hastened his speed, flapped his wings and landed on the bank.

Marlie's mouth dropped open. 'You mean they come when you call?' she demanded, incredulous.

Greg's look suggested she was demented. 'Of course! They've been tame for years. And they were born wild creatures, so we don't keep them penned.'

Marlie thought about the chaos in the factory, her problems with tying cords to their ankles and her fear when she thought the mallard drake had escaped.

'Oh-h-h,' she wailed in frustration. She looked down at her new outfit that had been, less than an hour before, so attractive. Her new sandals were ruined, and so was her perfect manicure. She wailed again. Then she glowered at Greg, her blue eyes flashing.

'Just don't speak to me ever again,' she ordered. 'At least not for the next five minutes!'

She stalked off across the yard, decided she could not enter the cabin in her condition, and turned towards the corner of the house and the hose.

Howard had anticipated her. He turned the nozzle to a medium-fine spray and caught them both unawares as they rounded the building.

CHAPTER EIGHT

MARLIE's second shower that afternoon was considerably more hurried. She dried her hair, and pushed it into a gleaming page-boy. Considering her record around Greg, she knew she was taking a risk by slipping into a pair of white linen slacks. But the blue-and-white sailor top was flattering to her figure and complementary to her eyes. The flat-heeled white sandals with tiny straps showed off her slender feet and ankles as well as the new shoes that were drying on the patio.

She applied her make-up with more than ordinary haste, but that evening she required less than usual. The exertions of scuffling with Greg in the river had brought to her complexion a glowing colour and her eyes sparkled. Was it the exercise? she wondered. She knew better, but decided she must not dwell on that. She was getting to know Greg too well. He had an uncanny way of finding the chinks in her defences. She needed to be on her guard every minute. She could imagine the string of broken hearts in his past, but when he sailed away on his yacht, she refused to weep for him. Wealthy men were used to collecting trophies, and not all of them with a gun, she surmised. This particular game was going to be completed without anyone being wounded, she determined.

While Greg showered, she joined Howard in the kitchen. He had already spread the table-cloth on the lawn table and had carried out the candles. While Howard arranged the dishes, glasses and flatware, Marlie diced garden-ripe tomatoes, cucumbers and onions, and washed lettuce for her salad.

From the oven, where they had been simmering undisturbed, she took the lima beans and combined the cream and mushrooms. While the last ingredients heated on top of the stove, she removed the stuffed pork chops, put them on a platter as she periodically checked the bread, and mixed her salad dressing. In that one field she could not outdo Henry, she knew, but she defied even him to improve on her mushroom stuffing.

When Greg strolled out into the yard, Howard followed him with the hot bread while Marlie checked the table for anything they had forgotten.

With his own clothing too wet and soiled to wear, he was dressed in a pair of Howard's cut-offs and a knit shirt. Greg was several inches taller than his host, but he was slim, and fitted the shortened jeans well. He more than filled out the shirt. Without the give in the material, he would not have been able to wear it at all. His broad chest, the muscles in his back and arms were outlined against the tight material. Below the frayed bottoms of the cut-offs, the dark hair curled on his tanned muscular thighs.

Wouldn't you know, Marlie thought. He could make even a ragged pair of old jeans look as if they were exclusively designed.

When Howard passed Greg the steaming platter of chops, he helped himself liberally and reached for the rolls. When Marlie had the time, she enjoyed making the cloverleaf clusters. That night they were golden and perfect.

'I'm getting to be a fixture at this table,' Greg said as he passed Marlie the limas with mushrooms. 'I may have to start paying board. Before I decide, what's for breakfast?'

'Duck.' She gazed at him solemnly over the top of her iced tea glass.

Howard grinned and bowed his head over his dinner. The gleam from Greg's deep grey eyes was ominous, but he made no reply.

'How long are the birds on vacation?' Howard asked.

'I'm having someone pick them up tomorrow at the boat,' Greg answered. 'That is, if they're not in the oven, and if I can get the cage in my car.'

'Why don't I put them in the back of the station-wagon,' Howard suggested. 'Doris and I are going into town tonight. I'll drop them off on my way.'

When dinner was over, Howard and Greg helped to clear the table. She was once again glad of the dishwasher. Several years ago she and her mother had threatened to hold a cook's strike unless it was installed. A vacation cabin was no place to spend hours washing dishes, they insisted.

She and Greg loaded the appliance and stored the food. Howard, mumbling about getting dressed, hurried to his room. While Marlie tidied the counters, Greg helped Howard load the ducks' wire cage in the wagon.

She had enjoyed his help in the kitchen. His breadth and height caused the rather large area to seem small and cozy. She heard the slamming of car doors and either one engine had stalled and had to be started twice, or he was following Howard back to the boat. Over the noise of the dishwasher, which had started roaring in its age, she couldn't be sure.

Better that he goes, she thought. Having him around for an evening could be dangerous to her heart, she knew. Still she was disappointed. After all her work and plans, surely he wouldn't leave without a word. She bent her head and scrubbed at a spot on the counter, trying to submerge her emotions under physical effort.

The roar of the appliance masked his entrance, so that she was startled by his voice.

'If you think you'll hand me a dishcloth, forget it.'

Did the room suddenly grow brighter? Marlie wondered. Afraid to turn, to let him see how his entrance affected her, she leaned over the sink, rinsing out the sponge. She laid it carefully on the small rack at the back of the counter.

'I thought you had followed Howard,' she said casually.

He stood in the kitchen door until she turned, and then he stepped back into the dimness of the screened patio.

Am I being manipulated? Marlie wondered. She was, she knew, but they could hardly continue to talk if he was outside in the dimness and she was in the kitchen. She followed, seeing him only as a dark silhouette against the silver of the moonlit water.

'Henry can look after the birds for a bit,' he replied to her question. He was still facing the water, but her shadow as she passed through the doorway had advertised her presence. He came to meet her. Marlie was aware of his tactics, but only because she was wary. His movements were so casual it seemed accidental that, with his natural breadth and his right thumb hooked in the pocket of the jeans, he had successfully blocked her way to the chairs at the other end of the narrow patio. Unless she pushed by him, she was forced to sit on the nearer end of the redwood lounge.

He was offering a challenge again, she thought. Something in her wondered if she had not been waiting for it, expecting and ready to welcome another battle of wits. This time she would be on her guard. She was not going to be caught with her defences down as she had been the week before.

But in that past week she had considered the man. He was much like the river that flowed by the cabin. Unless one knew it was part of a vast complex of channels and dredged streams, its depth could be deceptive and dangerous. But Marlie knew the stream, and after her experience on her walk, she thought she could handle Greg Alston. If not, she was only a hundred yards from where the Billings, next door, were cooking on their outdoor barbecue. She could see the glow of the charcoal and Mrs Billings moving around the small portable table in the light of candles.

But once she thought of it, running to the Billings for help was silly. Greg was not a man from whom a woman would have to force an escape. Nor was she sure she would want to.

She took the seat on the end of the cushioned redwood lounger. Greg dropped down beside her, his face turned away, looking south.

From that direction the sound of marine engines carried over the water. They sat in a companionable silence for several minutes waiting to see what type of vessel appeared around the bend.

Their wait was worthwhile. As if teasing the eye, offering an appetiser before a feast, lights twinkled between the trees on the other side of the river. They were in sight in intermittent patterns only to be hidden again by the foliage.

Then the first boat came in sight. The nautical running lights, the square gleams from windows, and the torchlit decks alerted Marlie to the treat in store.

'It's that convoy of houseboats,' she said as the second

vessel rounded the bend. 'They pass occasionally, but I've never seen them on the river at night. They're beautiful!'

She leaned forward slightly, watching the unhurried approach. Over the throb of the engines they could hear shouting and laughter. On the first boat, illuminated by the torchlight, two children were standing, waving towards the shore.

'Is it dangerous, running the waterway at night?' Greg asked.

Marlie was poised to say he should know, but she remembered he had a crew for his boat. With his busy schedule, he probably left the crew to move the boat from place to place. That's wealth for you, she thought with a tinge of contempt, and chided herself for being unfair. Rich or not, if he had no time to see the beauties of the waterway, he was to be pitied. She answered him with a genuine sympathy.

'I don't think so,' Marlie replied. The channel is well marked, and they travel through here often—see, there is the flash of his lights.'

From the first boat came a powerful beam of a searchlight. A long bright oval skimmed the surface of the water, pausing momentarily where the marker buoys indicated the channel. The light travelled quickly along the surface and was dimmed.

Both Marlie and Greg remained silent as the lights of the moving houseboats and their reflections on the water turned the silent river into a theatre for a light show. A quarter of a mile upstream several fishermen were trying their luck from the bank. Apparently, they gave up any idea of getting a strike while the boats were passing, so they abandoned their silence, calling out to the voyagers. The laughter and banter added to the party atmosphere.

Not until the nautical parade had passed did Marlie notice that Greg's arm was resting on the top of the cushion at her back.

'That looks like fun,' he said, his face finally turned in her direction. Until then she had not allowed herself to believe she had been waiting for his attention.

'Oh, I guess so,' she countered. It's a slow way to travel if you're going any distance. I doubt they have crew's quarters aboard.'

His expression was hidden by the darkness, but she saw the gleam of his white teeth as he smiled.

'Was that a shot across the bow? Have we broken the temporary truce?'

'Did we have one?' Marlie asked, surprised.

'I thought so, since we haven't had a pitched battle in ten minutes.'

Was that an attempt to start one? Marlie wondered. The darkness kept her from seeing his eyes. She tried to pick up his intent from his voice and failed. While he spoke with a pleasant inflection, his tone gave nothing away. A good negotiating voice, she thought. She leaned forward, picked up the matches she had placed on the table earlier, and lit the glass-enclosed candle.

His look, half amused, was slightly irritating to Marlie.

'If you think I was trying to start an argument, you're mistaken,' she said with unnatural primness. 'I've been aboard a few, and I hardly think they'd fit your lifestyle.'

He was very still, but Marlie sensed a withdrawal.

'I see. And you're convinced that I'm locked into my habits. I can't see past my nose, or enjoy anything different?'

'I hardly think you'd be comfortable without your crew and your Friday "gofor"—or whatever you call Henry.

Slumming it around a cabin on the river and going fishing in a boat with an outboard motor is a novelty right now, but you'll tire of it.'

She was half surprised at the flatness of his eyes, the set of his jaw. He was angry. Forcefully angry, but holding himself in. Marlie wished she could have taken back her words, but they were said, they were the truth.

His voice was low, dangerous. 'I'm glad you warned me. Now, when I grow bored, I can look back and remember you told me I would.' He stared at her for a moment, then looked out into the darkness beyond the candle. 'You surprised me. I didn't expect you to be a snob.'

'That's an unfair remark,' Marlie retorted. 'I'm not a snob because I'm not blind.'

'No, but there's a difference between blindness and deliberately distorted vision,' Greg replied through tight lips.

'Thank you,' Marlie's voice carried a touch of ice. 'Call it distorted if you want, but when you tire of hobnobbing with the local yokels, you'll return to your friends in New York and Paris, or wherever you spend your time. You'll go back to the beautiful socialites—' Marlie could have kicked herself for sounding like a jealous female. She could imagine his scorn. She flinched, expecting him to come back with a scathing remark.

The tiny muscle under his jawbone was quivering again. She knew she'd touched a sore spot on his ego.

'What am I, in your opinion—' he asked, then shook his open hand as if erasing his words. 'Don't answer that, I can read between the lines. In your mind I spend my time running over people, getting my own way, and ravishing virgins, looking for—what did you call it?—a speciality?

Perfection?' A heavy breath of suppressed rage hissed between his clenched teeth. 'Do we go on now to the wretched men I ruined in shady business dealings, or to the string of broken hearts that lie in my wake?'

His scorn, and his ability to know what she was thinking, sent Marlie's defences soaring.

'I don't know how many females you've left behind you in your search for perfection, or whatever the connoisseur's term is, but here you leave no broken heart. When you get back to New York and can't remember the name of that funny girl who painted ducks, you'll know she's one who has an equally short memory.'

'So I'll be forgotten before I'm out of sight?'

His face was flushed with anger, his eyes were narrowed to a dangerous gleam, but Marlie refused to be intimidated. Her chin came up.

She replied with an arrogance worthy of Scarlet O'Hara. 'You can believe it!'

In a sudden move, not taking his gaze from her face, he reached out and grabbed the candle. His piercing eyes, nearly black with rage, were the last she saw as he blew out the small flame. His voice cut through the sudden darkness:

'Like hell yóu'll forget me!'

His silhouette was a blur as he moved forward. His hands, hard and forceful, grabbed her shoulders, pulling her towards him until his lips found hers, bruising, bringing both pain and a demanding pleasure. Still holding her tight, he moved one arm around her shoulders and the other under her knees. She felt herself lifted and laid down on the soft cushions of the redwood couch.

In one fluid movement he was beside her, his long hard body pressed against her, trapping her with part of his weight. His hands, that less than a week ago had been so gentle in the awakening of her passion, were pressing hard against her flesh, kneading her side and leg, her arm, her breast.

Marlie gasped at her own reaction. She had been, that evening in the wood, like a sleeping thing slowly awakening to his gentleness. Now her body responded to his rough demands by flaring into an ecstasy of desire, into an urgency closely matching his.

No, she told herself, this is the very thing I must not do. In giving in to the desires of her body, in allowing Greg Alston to be the man to bring about that first unforgettable experience of true joining, he would gain a place in her life that could never be erased.

Her will struggled against her body but, even as she fought, her arms encircled his back, drawing him closer, joining him in his demands.

His lips left hers. His tongue found the secret tender places around her ears. His hand interrupted the torture of her breast to push back the boatneck collar of her blouse, where his tongue found the hollows of her throat, and travelled down towards her breasts.

She moaned as he teased her senses into a frenzy of desire. His hand moved down the outside of her thigh, and then started up again, caressing the more tender flesh on the inside of her leg. Still torn between her mind and her body, she knew her logic was losing the battle when, of their own volition, her legs parted to give access to his exploring hands.

Her body was an echo of her mind. So powerful was the passion he had aroused, that she was in terror of being drawn further into that strange territory. She felt as if she were on the edge of a strange and frightening sea. Something irresistible was pulling her forward, she could not withstand the beckoning, yet if she gave in, slipped into those unknown waters, would she ever leave them? The sea and Greg seemed to be demanding more than some bodily reaction—her heart and will were being pulled from her. Instinctively, she knew there was more involved than bodily lust, part of her would be consumed by him, and part of him would never leave her. Once she made that trade she was no longer a solitary being.

She mentally fought against him, terrified of unknown perils, yet physically she held tight, not daring to let go for an instant. Losing the promise offered by his growing urgency was a fear that loomed like a thundercloud of doom.

His hands stopped torturing her body and suddenly he pulled away from her, raising to one elbow as he tugged and worried with her blouse. He fumbled for buttons, and realising there weren't any, he was pulling it up when a laugh came from the Billings as they worked over their barbecued dinner.

His head turned in their direction for a moment. Then he was on his feet, lifting Marlie in his arms. He carried her into her bedroom and lowered her to the bed. Her arms were still around his neck, but once there he turned away. Shocked, stunned and disappointed, she raised on one elbow as she saw him outlined against the window. He was standing very still, looking out into the night. His chest still heaved with the ragged breathing of his passion. His jaw moved as if he were gritting his teeth.

'Greg?' she whispered, puzzled. He averted his face. She called his name again.

'You can call me what you will,' he rasped, 'but I've never taken any woman in anger.'

Marlie's mind was still spinning from his lovemaking. She had completely forgotten their argument. How did she answer him?

Before she could get her thoughts in order, he had left the window. She could barely make out the blur of the light shirt as he moved towards the doorway.

'This is not what I planned, not what I wanted,' he spoke through clenched teeth. 'And I won't let you goad me into it.' Open-mouthed, Marlie watched as he crossed the room, stumbling into a chair in the darkness. Then his tone changed. 'Tell Howard I'll be here in the morning.'

The white blur in the doorway was gone. Marlie sat up on the side of the bed. She wondered if she could trust her watery legs to follow him. She wanted to convince him that she understood.

Understood what? What had happened? Before she could make her mind and legs follow her heart, the engine of his sports car roared to life. The snarl that had been in his voice had been transferred to the car as he raced off into the night.

Marlie had never felt so alone. She had been right about that treacherous water. Only it had not taken the culmination of their lovemaking to rob her of part of herself. She felt as if she had lost something vital, something that made her a total person, and had been given nothing in return. Part of her was in that speeding car, it was with him, had melted into him. Though she could give it no name, it left a void that only part of him, left in return, could fill.

She collapsed on the bed, too miserable for tears. Her pain was too big for her—she was overwhelmed. It gagged her, blocking the release that might have lessened it.

Greg Alston had his souvenir. She could now name what he had taken. He might not remember the name of the duck lady in the boondocks, but he was too experienced not to know he had walked off with her heart. He had another trophy.

Marlie's misery was compounded by a difficulty sleeping. She was still lying awake when Howard came in. Several times during the night she awoke, weighed down under her misery. In her half-conscious state, she had trouble putting a name to it, but memory was never long delayed.

The next morning she was awake long before daylight. Knowing she wouldn't sleep again, she rose, and worked quietly in the kitchen preparing for breakfast. Greg would arrive too late to see her get flour on her face, but if she did it wouldn't matter to either of them, she thought.

During the night she worked out her own answer to what he meant by his cryptic remark. He said he neither planned nor wanted to make love to her, he simply was not interested. She had been a fool to think he was.

With wealthy and beautiful women trailing after him, he had no need to seek female companionship. Howard and a new fishing ground was what drew him to the cabin, she decided. She had been a recipient of his naturally charming and flirtatious nature, but that was all. It had been her ego that convinced her he would want, even as a trophy, the heart of a woman who covered herself with paint and mud.

'So much for you,' she muttered as she took her first cup of coffee out to her stump. The sky was just turning grey in the east. She wished she had time to drive out to the ocean and watch it rise. But sitting among her marigolds and zinnias, watching their colours emerge with the light, was a pleasure denied her when she was on the beach. Sitting on the stump was homy and safe.

Absently she ran her fingers over the rough wood. The great Greg Alston would probably describe it to a group of his cronies at a New York cocktail party, leaving everyone wiping their eyes after laughing at the joke. But it was her stump and she liked it.

She heard the throaty purr of the sports car. Greg was early, quiet as he closed the door of the car.

Marlie kept her eyes on the river, not daring to turn around. What would her face show? She had no idea if she knew how to hide her feelings. A broken heart, if that's what she suffered, was not in her field of expertise.

She heard Howard call from the kitchen window and Greg answer. She still didn't turn as they came across the yard. The lawn chairs were close to the flower-bed. Both men sat. Howard poured Greg a cup of coffee and called to Marlie to come for a refill.

She knew she had to go. Sooner or later she had to face Greg, and the less light, the less he could see. She made up her mind to stroll over, get the coffee and say something casual, inane.

She strolled over, held out her cup to Howard and gave Greg a nod.

'You're early.' That was inane.

'I am.' That was inane, too.

Glad of an excuse to get away, Marlie went to the kitchen. If Greg thought he was going to be surprised with something different for breakfast every time he showed up to go fishing, he was mistaken. Marlie liked to cook, she was imaginative in the kitchen, but never before ten in the morning. Breakfast was the same standby that had served her family for generations. The dieticians might frown on eggs, but nothing had more staying power. If the men were going to spend their day fishing, they needed food that would hold them through the morning.

The ham was sizzling in the pan, she had hulled some strawberries, mixing them with bananas and then adding the heavy cream. The farm-style biscuits were golden brown when she discovered there would be four for breakfast.

The put-put of outboard motors was no novelty in the early morning and she had paid no particular attention to the one that slowed and stopped in front of the cabin. But she smiled as Jonas Jones followed Howard and Greg into the kitchen.

'I haven't seen you this year, Jonas,' she said, handing him a cup of coffee. 'You'll have breakfast with us, of course.'

'Well, guess I could, no harm in one meal out—don't do it often, mind.'

Marlie nodded with forced solemnity. She was being afforded an honour, she knew. Jonas was by choice a hermit. His ragged clothing and torn sneakers made him appear a pathetic character, but he was proud and independent. Everyone on the river knew that few were considered by Jonas worthy of his conversation. If she could keep him for breakfast, she was sure his reaction to Greg would be interesting. Interesting to Greg, as well, if she knew Jonas.

They were halfway through breakfast. Howard and Greg were discussing the relative merits of various fishing spots when Jonas put down his fork, staring at Greg's shirt.

'Sell clothes, do you?'

Greg, who had just taken a bite of ham, nodded. Marlie

thought his reaction was a little too enthusiastic. If he was
condescending to Jonas, she would resent it, she knew, but
his attitude seemed only encouraging. Jonas leaned forward, taking a closer look at the shirt. Then he leaned
back, frowning.

'Couldn't sell that one, I take it.'

Marlie glanced at the dove-coloured knit shirt, obviously tailored by a name whose very existence was a secret
known only to the select few. Jonas wore a ragged green
tee-shirt that had begun life as a respectable under-
garment for a soldier. His trousers were a match, both in
origin and wear. While Howard choked, she ignored him,
holding her breath. If she dared breathe, her mirth would
be hysterical.

Greg, stunned speechless, had shaken his head.
Whether he was answering Jonas or expressing his wonder, she didn't know. But Jonas wasn't finished. He took
another close look and patted Greg on the shoulder.

'Good money in fishing.'

Howard left the table with a fit of coughing. Marlie
expelled one breath and drew in another. Her face was
beet-red from holding her breath, but she wasn't worred
about her appearance, as long as she could keep from
laughing.

Greg, with all his poise, his exclusive school training,
his jet set aplomb, stuffed an entire biscuit in his mouth to
stop any sound.

Marlie created a diversion by pouring more coffee.
Greg kept his eyes on his plate, and she was grateful. The
less eye contact she had with him, the more likely she was
to control her mirth. She was just sitting down again when
Howard returned to the table.

He tried to turn the talk into safer channels.

'What brings you out so early?' he asked Jonas.

'Trouble with my water pump,' Jonas muttered as he suspiciously eyed the dish of strawberries, bananas and cream. He had saved his fruit for desert.

Marlie met Howard's eyes. The flat statement, lacking any emphasis, held a tremendous importance to the few who knew Jonas. He needed help. He had, in his own way, asked for it. Nothing else would be said. Either he received it or he didn't.

Marlie knew, too, that Howard felt he must assist old Jonas.

'Do you want to take my boat?' she asked her uncle casually.

'No, better take mine,' Howard replied. 'I'll take tools, but we may have to bring the pump back here to the shop. You and Greg go on with your plans.'

Marlie's question had been unnecessary. She was only letting Greg know Howard was going with Jonas. The first part of Howard's answer was expected. The second part was not. He was saying she was to take Greg fishing. He couldn't know about their argument the night before, or what followed. She tried to catch his eye, but he had turned his attention to the old hermit, completely ignoring her.

Greg had held a still, listening silence, taking in the undercurrents of the conversation, she knew. He was a man too used to nuances not to understand. He was giving his concentration to his plate, leaving her and Howard to settle the arrangements.

Jonas thanked Marlie for a 'tolerable' breakfast, and left the kitchen when they rose from the table. Howard helped Marlie and Greg with clearing the table and fixing two large picnic lunches.

'Sorry, but I've got to go,' he muttered to Greg.

Greg nodded. 'We've got one just like him in Maryland,' he replied.

The sun was just up when they gathered at the slip. Jonas eyed the two coolers in Marlie's boat. The smaller one held cold water and canned drinks. The larger had ice and was to be used for the fish they caught.

'Too many weekenders out this morning,' Jonas said. 'I'd go to the graveyard.' He looked at Marlie under his eyebrows. 'You could get in—' He looked Greg up and down, taking in the shirt again. 'He couldn't.'

Marlie beamed under the praise from the old man. She had manoeuvred the treacherous path many times, but to have Jonas recognise her skill with a boat was a compliment bestowed on few. In saying Greg could not, he meant a stranger could and probably would find himself in serious trouble.

Marlie waited until Howard and Jonas had poled out into the river, started their outboards and were out of sight before she stepped in her boat.

The Whisk was small, only twelve feet in length. The thirty-five horsepower Evenrude motor would take Marlie anywhere she wanted it to go. She could not compete with the speedboats, but with no more than three people aboard, she could make considerable speed. Then, too, she had advantages denied the more luxurious vessels. Her motor lifted off, and could be locked in Howard's workshop when she was away from the cabin. While she had the power and speed to travel distances in a short time, her motor could be released and tilted if she found herself clogged by weeds or suddenly in the shallows.

But at the moment she wasn't thinking about her boat. Greg was lifting the hawser off the mooring post. She dreaded the day in his company, as visions of the night before kept intruding into her mind. How could she blot that out? How could she even attempt to act natural? He would probably pretend the evening never happened—but in that she was wrong.

He stepped into the boat, picked up the pole to push them out into the stream, and hesitated. Moving easily, showing his familiarity with boats, he took a seat while they were still drifting in the slip. His eyes were soft. A half-smile played on his lips.

'Pax,' he said softly.

'Wh-what?'

'Peace. Truce. I can't apologise for my feelings, for wanting you, but last night was unfair to both of us. We deserve something better. Let's start this morning with a clean slate—okay?'

Marlie nodded. She was surprised, confused, and glad she need not pretend. She felt some effort was due on her part.

'Do you want to take us out?' She waved her hand at the motor.

Greg drew back, feigning dismay. His eyebrows were arched as he fingered his collar.

'In this shirt? We'd never make it.'

CHAPTER NINE

MARLIE waited until Greg had poled them out into the stream. As they drifted lazily on the water, she adjusted the throttle and gave a tug on the starter cord. The motor roared to life. After letting it idle for a few minutes to warm up, she readjusted her throttle. The stern dipped as the propeller bit into the water. The bow of the light fibreglass boat lifted as they sped down the river.

Ahead, the reflection of the trees and plantlife on the edge of the placid waterway created a double world. No breeze ruffled the surface, and the disturbances of earlier boats had disappeared. In some places the banks, left by the dredging equipment, were still sharp cut, as if they had been carved only the day before. But where the sharp knife-like blades of cattail grass rose three and four feet from the water, the mirror image of growth seemed to extend out into the river.

Behind them the wake of the fast moving little boat spread out to the banks, losing its force on the way. Lazy little waves splashed against the water plants and brushed against the river banks.

They had travelled almost two miles downstream when they rounded a slight curve. Ahead, and just coming into sight, was a small ocean-going freighter.

'Slight detour!' Marlie shouted to Greg and whipped the tiller around, abruptly reversing her direction. A hundred yards down their wake was a wide creek she knew well. With no loss of speed Marlie headed into the tributary. She travelled as far up the creek as she dared, dropped her forward motion to trolling speed and made another complete turn. When she allowed the motor to idle, the bow was facing the river.

Her straight look at Greg was half defensive.

'Call me coward if you want, but I don't cross the wake of the big ladies.'

Greg nodded. 'Narrow here.' She saw understanding in his eyes. He drew the sturdy pole from beneath the seats and held it as he waited.

That one action told her he knew what they faced and what had to be done. Not only would she be spared any teasing, but he would be a help in holding the small boat when the large ship passed. He moved up to crouch in the bow. The hand that held the pole was relaxed, but he had dropped one end off the right side of the bow. He looked over his shoulder, and Marlie knew he watched her as she checked the catch that held the motor upright once it was attached to the boat. She reached under the seat, pulled out the emergency oar and laid it within easy reach, knowing she would need it later.

Satisfied that she knew her task, he turned back to watch for the bow wave. Few people ever gave a thought to the small disturbance at the front of the boat. Arching out from a small boat on the river, or a ship out in the bay, that white-topped curl appeared playful, lively, never frightening. But in those situations, the vessel was small in comparison to the surrounding volume.

What approached Marlie and Greg as they waited, bore no resemblance to a froth-capped wave. A good portion of the river water, trapped within its banks, was being pushed ahead of the ship. It piled and compounded upon itself, creating a visible hill of water, an artificial tidal wave. As it moved, the opposite bank disappeared under the rising tide.

When the sudden tide rushed into the creek, Marlie steadily increased the pressure on the throttle to keep the boat from being washed up among the trees. The banks, lower on that side of the river, were completely lost under the surging water. She kept her gaze fixed on two trees, using them as landmarks to stay in the middle of the stream.

She spared only a glimpse for the ship as the bow passed. She noticed the Liberian registration and heard the 'Halloo's' called in foreign accents. Had she been standing in the yard at the cabin, she would have tried to guess their nationality as she answered and waved, but at the moment she was occupied. Her next movement required all her concentration to achieve split-second timing.

Once the bow wave crested, the reverse flow would begin. Her gaze shifted back and forth between the trees that were her location reference and the bow of the ship. After years of watching such vessels pass she knew exactly when to expect the change in flow.

'Now!' Greg shouted to be heard over the ship's throbbing and the roar of the Evenrude, but Marlie had already cut the power. Working quickly, she released the catches and tilted the motor forward, bringing the shaft and propeller out of the water. She grabbed the emergency oar, thrusting it down and forward, ready to assist Greg in holding the boat against the pull that was coming.

As the bow passed, and with it the crest, left behind was an emptiness that showed the shallower original river bottom near the banks, left when the deeper channel was dredged. With the bow pushing water ahead, and the force of the powerful screws forcing water back behind the ship, the surface had visibly dropped several feet below normal.

The full creek emptied, its contents pouring into the emptiness that had only minutes before been a quiet river.

Greg threw his weight against the pole as he used his strength to keep the small craft from being swept forward. Marlie buried the tip of the oar in the creek bottom. Bracing herself, she held the stern in position, keeping it from spinning around on the pivot of Greg's pole. As the water rushed away, the small boat settled in the mud, tilting slightly.

Once the boat was grounded, Marlie was able to relax. In the bow, Greg's shoulders lost their tension, but he kept one hand on the pole.

'That's a weird sight, isn't it?' He spoke without turning around.

Marlie knew what he meant. For the water to suddenly drop several feet below its normal level was a departure from normal that upset the senses.

'It's not so spectacular where the river is wider,' she said casually. 'We are in a particularly narrow section.'

As the stern of the ship passed, the final step in the natural phenomenon approached. Some distance behind the ship, kept back by the powerful thrust of the screws, the river followed. A slope of water rolled over itself, filling the void the freighter left behind. Nature mending herself at the same speed as the man-made vessel, was in itself unsettling.

As the rolling wave passed, part broke away. Freed from the restraints of the propeller thrust, it rushed and bubbled in the creek bottom until the natural surface had been reached. Greg and Marlie, using the pole and the oar, held the boat to the centre of the stream until the peace of the quiet river was restored again.

Marlie pushed the motor up, lowering the propeller back into the water, and fastened the clamps. While she tucked the oar under the seat, Greg turned and did the same with the pole. His smile as he faced her was genuine. She was thrilled by the admiration she could see in his grey eyes.

'Hey, gal, you done good! Even Jonas would have approved.'

'You weren't so bad yourself—for a city slicker.' Her joking qualification of her compliment was an attempt to hide how deeply she had been affected by his praise and the way he offered it. He was generous, not begrudging her abilities, yet, by his actions in handling the pole, he had the knowledge to handle the situation as well, if not better, than she.

Marlie pulled the starter cord, adjusted the throttle, and ran the boat out on the river. After checking to make sure the way was clear, she swung out into deep water and increased her speed. Ahead, the leaves of the trees moved slightly in the light breeze, the waterbugs made widening circles as they moved along the surface, and the slanting rays of the sun added contrasts of shading to the reflection of the marsh growth and trees on the water.

Two miles further on, Marlie slowed her speed at what appeared to be the intersection of two rivers. Before the channel had been dredged, the original stream had meandered across the flat area of the tidelands, and some of the snaking curves had been ignored in favour of a less tortuous route.

Half a mile up the natural waterway, the river made a hairpin turn. To the left, the stream curved away, and three boats were anchored as anglers tried their luck. To the right, the water spread out into a small lake. Warning signs alerted fishermen to submerged obstructions.

Not all the obstacles were submerged. Rising from the acres of still water were the hulking shapes of rotting wooden barges. They created a nautical ghost-town of bows, hulls, and unsafe decking. Here and there a small cabin or pilot house tilted crazily, caused both by the cant of the half-sunken wreck, and its own rotting supports. As they approached, beneath the surface other wrecks were dimly visible in the murky water.

Marlie dropped back to her slowest possible speed and circled twice before attempting to enter the graveyard.

Greg, who had been twisting on his seat, inspecting the general area and the sunken barges close enough to see clearly, turned, grinning.

'That's a paradise.'

'If we get in,' she muttered, concentrating on locating her mental key. 'For me, getting started is the roughest part. Once I find the place I want to enter—there it is.' She sighed. To fail would be terrible, she thought, after bringing him this far.

Marlie had not been back to her favourite fishing spot that year, and during the winter storms or the autumn hurricanes, several of the wrecks had shifted. Once she located the barge that had once worn the name Old Sally, she knew her way. She was just relaxing when she saw Greg's worried expression. She wondered if he had decided not to trust her to take them through the obstacles, but he pointed behind them.

'I think we may have company,' he muttered. 'Those characters look like they want to follow.'

'Then they had better ride my wake,' Marlie replied, by

now concentrating on her course between two submerged wrecks. Not until after she spoke did she realise how arrogant she must have sounded. Her words had held a literal connotation a local would have understood. She had first learned to manoeuvre a boat through the barges by following close to Howard's boat, but she wondered if Greg recognised that. Looking back, she was relieved to see the fisherman in the stern of the other boat was refusing to make the attempt.

But what did Greg think? An effort to justify herself would make the situation worse. She tried to lessen the distasteful impression she was sure she had made.

'Do you see a spot you'd like to try?' she asked.

'You do the choosing,' he remarked as he turned his head from side to side, getting a good look at the area. 'I'll take your word for it.'

Was there anything sarcastic in that remark? she wondered. No. His head turned slightly as they passed within inches of some jutting planking, and she saw his absorption. He was relaxed, interested, and enjoying the ride, letting her use her own judgment without reservation. She had wondered fleetingly, as they passed the other fishermen, how he felt about a woman running the boat, while he sat idle. But she decided she had done him a disservice in thinking about it.

Greg Alston was a powerful and successful man. Too powerful and successful to find any other person's abilities a threat to himself. That was for lesser men. She thought back to little over a week before, when he had run the carving machine at the factory, and his assistance with the boat in the creek. He was too big a man to limit himself to only the larger things in life. He encompassed everything he could reach.

She warned herself not to think about that. He was beginning to look too good in her eyes, especially after his last words to her the night before.

She concentrated on manoeuvring the boat through the narrow, twisting channel. Marlie didn't consider her ability to traverse the dangerous area anything in which she should take a particular pride. No skill was required. A modicum of common sense, enough to keep the speed down to a minimum, and a memory for the twists and turns were all she needed.

She cut the motor as the boat entered an open area, letting it drift until they were in the centre.

'This spot okay with you?' she asked.

'Fine.' Greg lifted the anchor and lowered it slowly by the rope. His movements were designed not to frighten away the fish.

They floated in the centre of the best fishing ground in the area. She could count on her fingers the people who knew the way into the less accessible sections of the graveyard, so the waters were neither overfished nor disturbed by speedboats.

The closest humans were the anglers they had passed at the bend in the river, and Marlie had travelled more than half a mile since passing the warning signs. To the left and straight ahead, the green marshgrass and a few trees were visible beyond the wrecks, but no human habitation. Behind them and to the right, the old barges, some piled one on top of the other, created a peaceful, but eerie atmosphere, intensified by the reflection. Water spiders danced across the surface of the water, flying insects dipped to avoid the hovering dragonflies.

The busy world seemed many miles away. Even the barges, evidence of man's intrusion, had weathered until they too seemed a part of nature.

A sudden doubt shook Marlie. Would Greg understand her reason for bringing him to this particular spot, or would he think she had some other motive? After the incident the night before, would he think she was trying to regain ground that had been lost when he suddenly walked out?

Her cheeks were growing hot at the thought. She was wondering if she should make some excuse and find a less isolated spot when the peace was disturbed. Across the calm sheet of bright water, a silver flash broke the surface. A large bass gleamed in the sunlight as it arced at the top of its leap and splashed back into the water. Greg watched the widening ripples and spun around on the front seat.

'Why are we sitting here, doing nothing?' he lifted the two padded folding boat chairs and attached them to the wider, middle plank that served both as a brace and a seat.

'That's not going to give either of us elbow room,' she remarked, hiding her real objection. Sitting that close to Greg, with the memory of the night before still reeling in her head, would make it difficult to be casual. She felt a slight tremor course through her body as she thought about it.

But Greg was giving her no chance to put an alternate plan into action. He was shifting the coolers, the thermos of coffee, the fishing gear and tackle boxes. By the time he had finished, there was no place for Marlie except on the seat beside him. He held out a hand to assist her as she stepped over the folded boat seats and waited while he raised the padded back-rests.

When he sat beside her, necessarily close in the small boat, she knew she would be unable to keep her mind on her fishing. Looking sideways, under the brim of her fishing hat, she watched him as he seemed totally absorbed in checking his reel. His first cast was perfect, settling the fly directly over the spot where they had seen the smallmouth bass break the surface. Marlie was just raising her rod and reel, wondering if she could do half as well when Greg spoke.

'I'd take a cup of that coffee, if you're offering.'

'Sure,' Marlie laid aside her rod and turned to get the cups and the thermos. She filled two cups and sat back, feeling the warmth of his arm on the back of her seat.

'Your coffee, sir,' she murmured, waiting for him to take it.

At that moment his line gave a jerk, and he was all attention, playing the fish. Marlie put the coffee on the plank seat in the bow of the boat and reached for the net. Then she sat back, watching Greg play the fish.

He was using the special line Howard and Marlie kept on their reels. To them, the fish deserved as much of a chance as the man. Most mediocre fishermen could bring in a bass or a bluegill with no trouble at all. Pitting a man's one hundred and seventy pounds against a three to five pound fish was not sporting. They handicapped themselves by a light line so that one false move on their part, and the fish could—and often did—win the contest.

Marlie watched as Greg gave his complete attention to his task. His strong brown hands seemed almost relaxed as he held the rod in his left, his right on the handle of the reel. He seemed to be caressing the equipment, concentrating on every nuance of the fish's movement. Marlie watched him, aware of how convincing those hands could be, how sensitive, how strong.

Poor little fish, you haven't a chance, she thought, but

she was wrong. In trying to out-think his prey, Greg mistook the slackening of the line to mean the fish was tiring while it was apparently playing him. The line snapped and lay slack on the surface.

He hissed under his breath, stifling a swear, and Marlie saw his gaze cut to the corner of his eyes, watching to see if she would take advantage of the situation to tease him.

'Happens to the best,' Marlie said as casually as she could manage. By his stiffening he had known she was hiding her true thoughts. 'You wouldn't believe how many hooks Howard and I lose,' she added, and knew, even as she said it, she sounded false.

He thought she was laughing at him, but her mind had been on whether one try and loss on the small line would make him want to switch to heavier tackle. She would be accutely disappointed in him if he did.

'As you say, it can happen to anyone,' he said grimly. He moved his coffee to the top of the cooler by Marlie's left leg as he opened the tackle box, reaching for another hook and leader. 'What about you? Aren't you going to put out a line?'

'I haven't had a chance,' Marlie objected. 'First I poured coffee, and then stood by with the net. You didn't bring Henry, remember?'

Greg raised one hand in surrender. 'I take it all back. But the coffee is poured, there is no fish on my line, and now it's your turn.' He cast again, took a swallow from his cup and leaned back, putting his arm around Marlie.

She followed his example by sipping her coffee, and sat back after picking up her rod. Her voice, as she answered him, was deliberately light. It would not do at all for him to know how she was affected by that arm so close around her shoulders.

'Yes sir, of course, sir, I will endeavour to join in the activity—sir!'

The last sir carried all the force she put behind her cast. She had never been an expert at casting over her left shoulder, and she proved it immediately. As her line flew out and settled on the water, Greg's hat was attached to the hook.

Not another dumb day! Marlie railed at herself. She thought of several things that might take his mind off her gaffe, such as tipping the boat or throwing the lunch overboard, but the consequences that could follow were as unattractive to think about as having to face him. To get the dread out of the way, she turned to meet his mockery.

His eyes showed his amusement, but the rest of his expression was carefully solemn. With deliberate slowness, he removed his arm from around her shoulders, and took his rod in his left hand. With his right forefinger he touched his tongue and made a score mark in thin air.

'One for you—' He licked his finger again and made another mark. 'And one for me.'

Marlie shook her head in exasperation. 'Losing a fish is not on a par with snagging a hat. You're at least half a point up on me.'

'Five points, but who's counting?'

'I'll reel it in, you get the net,' Marlie grumbled and carefully worked the hat across the water.

'I will admit it was entirely my fault,' Greg said when they had recovered his hat and Marlie had attempted to blot it dry with a wad of paper towels. 'It was ungentlemanly of me to take the right seat. Please change with me.'

'Oh, no,' Marlie demurred. 'You are my guest. You remain where you are.'

Her next cast was more successful. They settled down

to await strikes and for a while they sat in a companion-able silence.

Marlie was having difficulty concentrating on fishing. Greg's proximity, his arm thrown casually across the back of her seat, the occasional touch of his leg against hers as he shifted his position, all brought back with vivid clarity the incident of the previous evening.

He had declared a truce that morning, and by all apparent expressions, inferences and conversation, he was keeping it. Still, she was bothered by his closeness.

As if he had been reading her mind, and some perverse-ness in his nature had decided to put her to a test, he shifted so he was facing her at an angle. Under the brim of his hat, his eyes were shaded and dark, but glints of light reflected off the water made her wonder at the thoughts behind them.

'I like this place,' he murmured softly. His voice was like a caress. 'I like having it to ourselves.'

Was there some meaning behind the last remark? she wondered. The muscles in his left arm, resting partly on her shoulders and partly on the back of the seat, were moving slightly, as if his hands or fingers were in motion, but without turning, she could not see, and they weren't touching her. His left leg, bent slightly, brushed her knee rhythmically as the boat was rocked by a breeze.

Marlie was not sure how to answer him. There seemed to be a particular meaning behind his words and position, but what if she were wrong? The night before he had told her he had not intended to make love to her. She had been fooled and hurt by misreading him once, and twice would be too much.

'I like coming here,' she said. 'It's no fun getting settled to fish and then being buzzed by speedboats.' That, she thought, should help keep the conversation on an even keel.

Greg reached for his cup again, leaning forward, his arm still around her shoulders, his face coming close to hers. She dropped her eyes, not wanting to see the golden-brown face, the strong jaw, the full, sensitive lips so near, yet so achingly far if she had understood his harsh words the night before.

She wondered if he could be playing some game, or if he had no idea of his physical attraction, but that was absurd. He was an intelligent person. It wasn't conceit to be aware of one's effect on others; only the very foolish or the coy pretended otherwise. But if he knew, then he was deliberately baiting her, as he had in the woods, as he had only the night before. But the night before they had both lost control of their emotions. Today she was on guard against that, and he seemed to be also. He had given her no reason for anger, just as she was giving him none. We're both walking on eggs, she thought.

Quite possibly, she would have felt better if they had stayed in sight of the fishermen at the bend in the river. They were so isolated, and his nearness was torturing her with memories of his caresses. She flicked the rod, watching the whip action as the line arced over the water. A strike would at least draw her attention away from him.

She kept a firm hold on the cork handle of her fishing rod and dropped her eyes. In front of her his long legs stretched out across the cooler, his left knee only a fraction of an inch from hers. She shifted, trying to relieve the tinglings his proximity sent coursing through her, while at the same time, afraid any movement might communicate to him her feelings.

He leaned forward again, drawing closer as if moving in

for a kiss, but only reaching for the coffee cup. Marlie's nerves tensed and relaxed. He was aware of it.

'Was it a strike?' he asked lazily, a slight curl of amusement on his lips.

'I thought so,' Marlie answered, glad he had at least given her a plausible reason for her reaction, even if he didn't believe it. Then she asked herself what right he had to give explanations for her behaviour with that smug look on his face. She wasn't having that.

'It was just a feint,' she added. 'Nothing to get upset about.' If he didn't catch the double meaning, he was pretty dense.

'They can be irritating, getting you ready for a move and then finding nothing to fight.'

Was he talking about fish? Maybe he was playing a cat-and-mouse game again, but did she dare accuse him of it? What a fool she would look if he denied it.

He leaned close again, putting his cup down. Behind his ear, his dark hair curled slightly. The deep brown that showed beneath his hat caught the sunlight, showing up several strands that gleamed a dark auburn. The softness of the wave made her fingers itch to touch and smooth the few pieces that had been disarranged by the breeze.

As if he knew what she had been thinking, when he straightened, he removed his hat, reaching across her to put it within reach of his left hand. For a moment she had been within a loose embrace. She tensed and relaxed again, this time more visibly than before.

'Another try at the hook?' he asked.

'Um-m-m,' Marlie nodded, at first not sure she could trust her own voice, but the gleam in his grey eyes assured her he was not referring to a fish. Still, if she accused him of anything, he could laugh at her.

'That little fish had better be careful,' she said. 'If he keeps playing around that hook, he's asking for trouble.'

'Then you think he might get what he deserves?' Greg asked.

'Let's just say he might get more than he expects, and it might not be at all what he had in mind.'

Greg's eyes glittered with amusement, but at that moment a large bass struck his fly and the line zinged out. He was busy for almost quarter of an hour, working the three-pound bass in on the small line, but this time he made no mistakes.

Marlie had to admit she had never seen a fish better played. Once it broke water she had warned him he had little chance of getting it to the boat and netting it on the thin filament they were using, but his skill and delicacy won the contest.

The next strike was on Marlie's line. After a stiff battle that lasted some minutes her line fouled on a snag, and she lost thirty feet of line as well as her hook, fly and leader.

'Another for you,' she conceded to Greg as she reeled in her line.

'That one doesn't count—hazard on the field,' he said.

After the brief flurry of activity, quiet again reigned on the still water. Greg poured more coffee, putting the cup back on the cooler.

The fish had given Marlie a respite, but after the two strikes, nothing seemed awake beneath that sheet of still water. Only Greg seemed to be restless, reaching for his coffee, checking the anchor rope, taking his hat off, and putting it on, and every action seemed to be designed to keep Marlie on the edge of her emotional seat.

Her senses were reeling from having him so near. As he leaned forward and across her to pick up the coffee again, his aftershave was tantalising in its dry meadows freshness. His strong hand, encircling the fragile styrofoam cup, reminded her of the passion she knew was in him, and the urges he had raised in her kept fighting to come to the surface.

His lips neared hers as he put down the cup. They were shaped in a relaxed sensuality of enjoyment. Her own tingled with remembered sensations. She pulled them tight against her teeth, not wanting him to read her thoughts in their trembling.

Each time he moved, Marlie wondered if he were going to renew the advances of the night before. Her nerves were screaming when he suddenly sat up, reeled in his line and stowed the rod and reel under the seat. Propping his feet up again, he slid down on the cushioned boat seat and lowered the brim of his hat until it covered his eyes.

'Wake me by two-thirty,' he mumbled. 'We'll have to start back by then to get ready for the party.'

'Wake you? What party?'

'Oh, didn't I tell you? Kara Holmes is having a party aboard their boat tonight. I told her we'd come. If you'll excuse me, I'll get some sleep.'

Marlie's fingernails dug into the cork handle of her fishing rod. Either he was stark, raving mad, or she was. How dare he tell someone she would attend a party without consulting her?

And how dare he give her those sultry looks, those innuendoes, almost touching, almost embracing, bringing her emotions to screaming heights, and then just go to sleep?

CHAPTER TEN

'I AM not going!' Marlie said as Greg raised the anchor and moved to the back of the boat to start the motor. He had slept away the afternoon on the uncomfortable boat seat and was in no mood for an argument. Disdaining to wake him, Marlie had allowed him to sleep until four-thirty.

She had to direct him out of the graveyard, but she sat in a stony silence until they were back at the cabin.

'I am not going to that party!' Marlie said as he strolled into her bathroom. She had to follow him since he had a firm grip on her hand. Luckily her make-up was confined to the one case she carried back and forth to town. He picked it up, marched her out to his car, and they sped away.

The louse! How had he learned her address?

'I am not going!' Marlie insisted as she stood in her bedroom while he sorted through her dresses and chose one. In self-defence she grabbed undergarments, shoes and stockings, and shoved them in a small carrying case. She knew he would choose for her if she didn't. By this time she was doubtful of winning the argument, but she kept trying.

'I am not going!' Marlie stood in the companionway on his yacht while he pointed imperiously into a stateroom.

For the first time he replied to that statement.

'Would you like some help with your shower?' The gleam in his eye, the determined set of his smiling mouth sent her scuttling inside where she slammed the door. She had lost this argument from the beginning, and she knew it.

The adamant objections she had repeated were only for show. She was glad she was going to the party—not that she cared about Kara and Bill Holmes, but Greg's insistence that he was going to take her had to mean something. It meant she was more in his mind than just a niece of a fishing buddy—or did it? Was it more? He couldn't be pulling some trick on her, could he? No, she wouldn't accept that.

She pushed the catch on the door and turned towards the shower. After her day on the river, getting clean and fresh again had definite attractions.

Marlie was just leaving the shower when Henry brought her a tall glass of iced tea. She enjoyed the leisure of drying her hair by combing it, since they had forgotten her hair dryer. Her small amount of natural wave, unconfined by the strictures of dryers and curlers, framed her face in tiny waves of fine hair and fell to her shoulders in a page-boy.

Since Henry had told her dinner was still some time away, she took particular care with her eyeshadow, blending white, brown and blue in faint and subtle shadings. It took time to achieve that perfection of enhancement and still keep a naturalness to the blended tones.

She was glad she thought to bring her sheerest stockings. But she wondered about her choice of shoes. They were high-heels, and never intended to be worn aboard boats. She slipped them on. Never mind, if necessary she would take them off.

Her dress was perfect. Teal-blue silk, it brought out the

blue in her eyes, deepening the colour and showing off her skin to perfection. Standing in front of her closet, Greg had reached for it unerringly, as soon as he saw the colour. The connoisseur, she thought, and pushed that unwelcome idea away.

Since she was going to the party, and would be spending the entire evening in his company, it would be foolish to begin another fight.

When she was satisfied with her appearance, she packed away her fishing clothes and went into the salon.

Dinner *grâce à* Henry was superb. The conversation between Marlie and Greg was desultory. He complimented her on her dress, a praise she could believe was genuine by the light in his eyes. He was the epitomy of elegance in his white dinner jacket. His tall muscular figure, and his rugged, dark good looks were an asset no tailor could build in.

Marlie was sorry to be leaving his boat when they crossed the deck, preparing to make the short walk down the pier to the Holmes' craft.

She was just putting her foot on the gangway when she heard a familiar sound. She looked up at Greg in surprise.

'I'd know that voice anywhere! That's Caesar!'

Greg nooded. 'You have a good ear for ducks.'

'I thought you were sending them back to your farm.'

'Slight hitch in plans. Minor problems on the farm are keeping everyone busy right now. I may be too cautious of those birds, but I'm not sending them by common carrier.'

'Are they comfortable on the boat?' Marlie was concerned.

Greg laughed. 'Comfortable? Caesar's elected himself admiral.'

Marlie had never considered herself particularly adept at eye measurements, but it was easy to see the Holmes' yacht was smaller than Greg's. Even from a distance the difference in the condition of the two vessels was apparent. Both boats represented a small fortune in teak alone, but aboard the *Veronica,* the constant care kept the surfaces a glistening gold. On board the *Windswept,* several spots of the decking showed a grey, weathered look. Marlie saw Greg's jaws tighten as he ran a hand over a wooden railing.

But the lack of care for the boat was not extended to the party. Lights were strung from the masts and yardarms, a red carpet had been spread out on the deck for better footing, and waiters were wandering about with trays of drinks and hors d'oeuvres. One glance at the trays of glasses showed her choice to be champagne, champagne, or champagne.

She was being put in her place already, Marlie thought. In her lack of sophistication, she had never acquired the taste for the effervescent wine. Greg lifted two glasses from the tray of a white-coated waiter and grinned.

'Carry this until I find the tea vendor.'

They had walked less than three paces across the deck when out of the crowd came Kara Holmes, a vision in silvery chiffon and diamonds at her throat, wrists and ears.

'So glad you could come, darling,' she said to Greg, linking an arm through his. 'How are you this evening—Marlie?' There was just the slightest hesitation before the name.

'Delighted to be aboard,' Marlie replied with a smile. The deeply veiled insult had not passed Greg, she saw, and his eyes sharpened.

Her next play will be to tell him there's someone he really must see, Marlie thought.

Kara, taking Greg's hand that held his champagne, lifted it, sipping from the glass. 'Darling, there is someone you really must meet, and here comes Lyle to entertain Marlie.'

Kara's hand raised, along with her voice, an obvious signal across the boat. Lyle's head came up as if he had received a stage cue, and he seemed to tilt as he came through the crowd. He had begun his partying early. Despite Greg's dislike of the man, Marlie saw no real harm in him. He was, she thought, one of those weak characters who seemed always to hang on around more energetic, successful people.

Remembering Greg's reaction the first time she met Lyle Kearns, she glanced at her escort. Kara had been as subtle as a raging bull, and Greg could hardly blame her because their hostess had called Lyle over. If he actually objected to the man she felt he was responsible for seeing to it that she was in other company, preferably his.

But his attention had been sought by two men. The first was slightly loud, a blustery character who managed to get an important name into every sentence. The second, smaller and nondescript in comparison to most on board, displayed a casual silence. By the genuine respect Greg afforded him, she knew she had been right to think he was someone above the ordinary.

Her idea of an enjoyable evening did not include Lyle Kearns, but the quiet man gave her pause. If Greg was attending this party for business reasons she could hardly hang on his arm. To stand in the way of a valuable contact he might make would be unthinkable. She resigned herself to being entertained by Lyle.

'Hel-lo,' Lyle flipped some inner switch, turning his smile on bright. He slipped an arm around her waist and bent to speak softly in her ear. 'Was there room for that one word?'

'Just barely,' Marlie replied. The rest of her quip died on her lips. Greg chose that moment to turn back to her. She saw his mouth tighten.

To her his disapproval was childish. If he wanted her by his side he could say so. Instead, he allowed himself to be led away by Kara. Disappointed, Marlie allowed her attention to be drawn by Lyle, who had snagged a full glass of bubbly from a passing waiter. He sipped and held up the glass, inspecting it critically.

'Ah, southern fried,' he murmured with appreciation.

'The secret is in the buttermilk,' Marlie volunteered.

Lyle cocked his head, looking thoughtful. 'A great mystery of life. How does one milk butter?'

'With both hands.'

Lyle took another sip from his glass and eyed her critically. 'I knew the moment you walked on board, the evening would come alive.' He took her arm and steered her to a pair of empty chairs on the fantail.

'You knew the minute I walked on board that Kara would snap her fingers and you were to keep me out of her hair,' Marlie retorted. Her remark was too blunt for good manners, she knew, but Kara's cavalier treatment still stung.

Lyle gave her a satanic smile. 'But did you ask yourself why it was necessary?' He seemed to find some secret amusement in his own words, but the meaning had eluded her. Then he shrugged.

'Hangers-on take orders,' he explained. 'They do their

bit—that is, if they want to keep riding around on the boat belonging to big brother-in-law.'

'Then Kara is your sister?' There was certainly no family resemblance.

'Unfortunately.'

'I'm sorry, I—' Marlie halted in confusion, feeling her cheeks heat up in embarrassment. One did not commiserate with another because of the other's relatives. She stumbled for a change of subject and blurted out a question that could be as ill-mannered, but one that had been on her mind for some time.

'Why are you down here—I don't mean you individually, but Kara and Bill, Greg, and the other large yachts? We like our part of the country, but we're hardly the centre of élite society.'

Lyle shrugged. 'Yachts are social creatures; park two together and soon you have four. We're here because of Alston. Bill wants to interest him in one of his schemes.'

'And Greg?'

'Originally the shipyard. He's been in and out, watching some repairs on the *Veronica*. Since the work was finished a week or so ago, maybe you can answer your own question. Obviously he's given up any idea of going into the hotel business—no matter how things look at present.'

At first, the last part of Lyle's comment went right over Marlie's head. She glowed inside at his hint that she could be the reason for Greg's remaining on the *Veronica*. But his eyes warned her.

She looked up as Greg came out of the salon with Joan Owens-Lane on his arm. Behind them, Kara Holmes looked smug.

Marlie gathered her courage and was about to rise, planning on brazenly joining the group, when she caught Greg's eye. His anger blazed as he looked in her direction.

How dare he, when he had another woman on his arm, she thought. To be truthful, she had to admit he wasn't hanging on to Joan, she was doing the clinging, but for him to give Marlie a hard look while he stood with Joan was just too much.

She turned back to Lyle, giving him an engaging smile. Out of the corner of her eye she saw Greg's glare, before he bent to hear what Joan was saying.

Marlie spent most of the evening in the company of Lyle Kearns. Joan and Kara seemed to be conspiring to keep Greg away from Marlie, and from her vantage point, they were getting little resistance from him. From time to time she let her eyes wander in his direction, but he was usually deep in conversation.

She was surprised, therefore, that while the party was still in full swing, he freed himself from Joan and came striding across the deck.

The anger she had seen in his eyes was still smouldering. He was curt with Lyle.

'Sorry to break this up. We have to be on our way.'

Lyle, who had been increasingly dull company after numerous glasses of champagne, nodded languidly, tried to rise and slid back in his chair.

'Come anytime, glad to have you,' he mumbled, staring out over the water with a glassy look.

With a firm hand on her elbow, Greg led Marlie down the ramp, along the pier and back to his car. He slammed both doors and spun the wheels as he left the parking lot. His hands were gripping the steering wheel, and his jaw was tight. Marlie could see that betraying little muscle as it quivered just below his jawbone.

He was out on the street when he made his first acid comment.

'I hope you thoroughly enjoyed your evening with Lyle Kearns.'

'Beautiful!' Marlie retorted, meaning his remark and not her evening. 'You spent all your time with your platinum girl-friend and ignored me completely. If you wanted to be with her, why did you invite me?'

'I wasn't aware she was in town,' he snapped.

Marlie jumped on that remark. 'But if you had known, you would have taken her, so I think you should be grateful I stayed out of your way.'

'That is an idiotic remark,' he growled.

'Then maybe I had better not make any more,' Marlie retorted.

As the low slung sports car sped around corners in the city and then on to the curving roads that led back to the waterway, Marlie sat tense. So much for hoping they would have a beautiful romantic evening. That had been a pipe dream, and she was foolish for letting it enter her head. Obviously she and Greg Alston were never going to spend more than a few hours together without friction.

She leaned back, turning her head slightly to watch him as he drove. He handled a car with his characteristic expertise. His strong brown hand lay on the gear shift. She could still see the tension in his fingers, but his driving was not influenced by his anger.

Could he really be jealous? she wondered. No, she decided. He had expected her to hang on to him as Joan had done. His ego was damaged because his friends discovered there was one female who wasn't falling all over him. An objection kept trying to creep into that line of thought, but she obstinately resisted it. He was an insufferable boor, she told herself, and held on to her thought. She waved it in front of her mind, like a cape in front of a bull. Better that than to be crushed by other considerations.

She had been so deep in thought she had not realised they were in familiar territory until Greg brought the car to a stop behind the cabin. He pulled up beside the battered station-wagon as Howard was opening the passenger door for Doris.

Greg threw her one last angry look.

'The next time we go out, I hope you'll stay away from Lyle.'

He was out of the car and walking around it before she could frame an answer. When he opened her door, she was ready.

'The next time we go out, volcanoes will be freezers,' she said, sliding away from his hand, held out to assist her.

'Nice party?' Doris called as Howard greeted Greg.

'Marvellous, but I've developed a headache and I'm going to bed,' Marlie answered. As she expected, Greg was about to accept Howard's offer of a nightcap, but under the circumstances he could only refuse.

She entered the house and was just switching on the light in her bedroom when she heard the sports car pull away. She had taken honours on that last round and kept him from staying. He had left angry. Would he ever come back? Do I care? she asked herself. No! she shouted her answer. Did she want to see Greg Alston again? No! No! No! She was lying to herself, and she knew it, but if she lied enough, it might become truth. At the moment that seemed the less painful course.

Sunday she moved listlessly around the cabin, taking care of small chores and making an effort to enjoy the beauties of the river. Somehow, with neither Greg nor the ducks sharing her afternoon, nothing seemed as vibrant, as colourful. Colour everything sad, she thought, then chased away that idea.

She hated and detested, simply loathed Greg Alston, and hoped she never saw another live duck! For the next half-hour she sat brooding on all the embarrassments she had suffered because of him and his pets. Feeling better, she went back into the cabin. But the lighter mood had been built on a false foundation. During the night, the rain, beating on the roof, seemed to add weight to her misery.

Monday morning Howard was getting ready to drive to the factory, and Marlie was planning to stay at the cabin. Howard was just leaving the kitchen when they heard the ragged put-put of Jonas's motor.

'That makeshift repair didn't hold up,' Howard said. 'We'll have to run over to Portsmouth and get a replacement part.'

'Want me to go in and open up?' Marlie asked, getting to her feet.

'Let me make sure I'm right first,' Howard grinned and went to meet Jonas.

Howard's assumption had been correct. In minutes Marlie was in the station-wagon, on her way into town. Fred had recently lost his key, so he, Paul and Norm would be standing on the pavement until she arrived.

The big push to get out the back orders was over, and that morning the three men were giving the small factory a good cleaning. Marlie helped move a few odds and ends, but her co-operation ceased when she walked over to the painting area. One look at the floor in front of her table, and she gave out with a spate of complaints against Greg

Alston, Paul and Norm, who had cleaned up the paint spilled when the ducks escaped, and men in general. The boys had scrubbed and sanded until not one trace of the original spill remained, but they had worked with extreme care, leaving every little webbed footprint intact. She was still giving the grinning boys her opinion of their work when a big brown truck, bearing the insignia of the transcontinental package delivery service, pulled up outside.

'If that's more ducks—' Marlie growled and went to meet the driver. He entered without the customary clipboard.

'Returned shipment,' he said. 'It's a big one—no idea what happened, but two of the boxes are damaged.'

Marlie walked out with him, looking in the back of the truck, which was filled with boxes.

'The Alston shipment,' she said, surprised.

'We can fill out the forms, I'll take it back and have it shipped on if you want,' the driver said. 'But a couple of the boxes took a pretty good beating. You might want to look at them.'

'Yes, let's unload them,' Marlie said. 'We'll want to replace anything that's been damaged.' Marlie took a look at the address labels as the driver rolled them in. By some mistake they had been delivered to a Mrs Anne B. Franklin in Tallahassee, Florida. The mental picture of a startled housewife facing one hundred and eighty wooden ducks was mind-boggling.

Forty-five minutes later, the cleaned production area was a jumble of boxes, styrofoam peanuts and wooden ducks. Five of the boxes, each holding six decoys, had been crumpled in shipping, but none of the carvings had received a scratch.

Fred straightened, rubbing his back after bending over the boxes.

'No point in opening the others. These are okay, and those boxes weren't even scratched.' Norm laughed. 'I'm just glad these are the wooden ducks. I'd hate to have this many live ones here.'

Marlie was very still, both mentally and physically. In her fertile brain an idea was forming. Greg Alston liked ducks. Live ducks and wooden ducks. And, after all, these were his, he had paid for them. He had ordered them, at least. She imagined his salon on the boat, his staterooms, his dining room, all loaded with decoys. After their last argument, she might never see him again, but if he were forced to bring back the shipment—

'Open all the boxes,' she shouted, startling the three men. 'Norm, do you still have that van?' She saw his nod. 'Paul, I didn't see yours this morning.'

'I sold it to my younger brother.'

That was a foul-up in Marlie's plan. She needed another vehicle, one that would hold a number of large boxes.

'Well, hire it back! Him, too, if you can get him.' Fred was watching her warily as Paul rushed to the phone. 'What are you going to do?'

'Play boss for a while, so don't argue with me,' Marlie laughed. 'If Howard comes in and starts yelling, refer him to me. I'm getting good at ducking—no pun intended.'

CHAPTER ELEVEN

WHILE Fred watched, prophesying doom for the factory, the employees and particularly Marlie, the rest fell to with a will. They ripped open the boxes and pulled the carved birds from their nests of styrofoam and packed them closely together in other boxes.

By the time the station wagon and the van was full, Paul's younger brother, Sam, had arrived. Marlie led the way to the marina, driving the station wagon. Behind her, Norm in his van, and Paul, riding with his seventeen-year-old brother in the second, followed.

Luck was with Marlie. Greg was out on business. The elderly deck-hand who seemed to be the only member of the crew, recognised Marlie. He told her that since Mr Alston had taken the car, Henry had ordered a taxi and left to do some shopping. He eyed the boxes Marlie and the boys carried on board.

'I don't know about cargo,' he said, shaking his head. 'We've never carried cargo that I can remember—and I've been aboard the *Veronica* for forty-five years—'

'But he wants these, that's why he's been staying around this area,' Marlie said. 'And he wants to see them. It seems he doesn't care much for our new painter, and he insists on checking the quality for himself.'

'You know how he is about quality,' Norm, who was enjoying the joke, added his bit.

That decided the old seaman, who stepped back out of their path.

'The salon first,' Marlie called and led the way. With

Norm unloading one box, and she another, they had already begun to cover the tables, chairs and couches with decoys.

'Can I put one here?' Norm pointed to a silver bowl, and suited action to words by placing a duck in it so it appeared to be swimming.

'Excellent,' Marlie replied, thinking of Greg Alston's face when he returned to the boat. She would teach him to make fun of her painting. She'd pay him back for all his smart insults. She'd also have to dodge his anger when he came around again. Remembering their arguments, and the result of one, she shivered in anticipation mingled with dread.

Paul came in, staggering under a large box, and behind him, his younger brother peered around the load he was carrying.

Norm, digging in the bottom of his almost empty box, looked up.

'Avast there, mate,' he said to young Sam.

'What's avast?' Sam asked.

'It means unload,' Marlie said, pointing to the dining room. She grabbed the edge of her empty box and rushed out, heading to the car for another load.

She unpacked hurriedly, removing the papers from the decoys. The boys were working just as fast. But when Norm disappeared with an empty box and was back almost immediately with a full one, she looked at him in surprise.

'That was quick.'

Norm grinned. 'I don't think that old guy trusts us. He's getting the boxes out of the vans, making sure we don't carry any away, I think. Or maybe he's just helping to be sure the boxes we take out are empty.'

Marlie paused, worried, but she couldn't stop her giggle. 'I hope he doesn't tell Greg he helped us.'

The *Veronica* was a yacht large enough to draw attention in any harbour, but like all ships, the living quarters were limited. One hundred and eighty wooden ducks, each nearly twenty inches in length, made a noticeable addition in the decor. Ducks sat on the dining room table, on the sideboard and nested in the chairs. Duck heads peered out from behind the throw cushions on the couches in the salon, perched on the footstools and wooden heads appeared over the top of the magazine racks.

In the staterooms they sat on beds, in chairs. Someone had been very creative, she thought. The upturned duck-tails were just visible as they stuck out from beneath the bedspreads that came within an inch of the floor. In the bathrooms they sat in the sinks, looked out of the showers. When she went back up the companionway, Paul was clustering a few on the carpet.

'Migration,' he grinned as he stood up.

'Let's get out of here,' Marlie said. 'I wonder how soon we'll hear from the great Mr Alston.'

'I don't know, but I'm going to stay out of the way, Paul chuckled.

They were still panting from their exertions when they walked down the gangway and over to the trucks. Marlie saw the taxi pulling away. Henry had returned. He carried two large bags of groceries, and had given two to the old sailor.

'I hope we're not in for it,' Marlie whispered to Paul. She could see the old seaman talking to Henry.

'Henry, I left your kitchen alone,' Marlie said, 'but I sincerely hope you'll allow Mr Alston to inspect his merchandise.'

Henry stood quite still for a moment, the concern and amusement striving in his expression. Training won out. His face was bland, unreadable.

'Very good, Miss Richmond, since I really must use my facilities. Mr Alston is at present at the airport, meeting a gentleman whose good offices are vital to a rather large business venture Mr Alston has in mind. They are due here for luncheon.'

'What!' Marlie cried out. 'Henry! Under all that gibberish, you're telling me he's going to be holding a business conference—'

Marlie wanted to sink in the sand. To play a practical joke on a man who was vacationing on a pleasure craft was one thing, but to risk making him look a fool when he was conducting a business deal was another and far more serious matter. She might storm and rail at his teasing her, but after all, he had done nothing to endanger her career or harm Howard's business. She had no right to treat him that badly.

She whirled to stop Paul and Sam before they closed the doors on Sam's van.

'Back to the boat!' she shouted, grabbing an empty box.

'I knew you would understand,' Henry murmured, trying to hide his smile.

Marlie dashed back towards the yacht, the box bumping against her leg. Behind her she heard other hurried footsteps and Sam's puzzled voice.

'I thought we avasted everything,' he panted.

'Now we unavast,' Paul retorted.

'Disavast, it's faster,' Marlie called, nearly falling over the box as she stopped just inside the salon.

Pulling the protective paper from the decoys had been a simple task. Wrapping them again was more difficult. In trying to hurry, Marlie dropped one duck twice, thankful that it fell into an upholstered chair. Norm, who was working in the same room, picked one up by the tapering tail and stared as it shot out of his hand like a bar of soap.

'Who greased them?' he demanded.

'We're just nervous,' Marlie said, biting her lip in an effort to grab a decoy, wrap it in paper, and lay it in the box, all in one smooth motion. She felt as jerky as a doll on strings, handled by a novice puppeteer.

From the dining room, she could hear Paul exhorting his brother to more speed. Sam was retorting by saying Paul was doing no better.

Marlie looked up as she saw Henry standing in the doorway. His eyes were crinkled with worry as he glanced at his watch.

'Henry, what are we going to do?' Marlie wailed. 'We'll never get them off in time. We can't just throw them in the boxes, if we ruin them, my uncle will kill me!' She pushed a wayward strand of hair out of her face. 'And Greg will kill me if I don't,' she muttered.

'We could hide them and come back later,' Norm offered. 'If we put them somewhere just for the afternoon, we won't have to wrap them. That'll save time.'

Marlie felt a surge of hope. 'Henry, are the guests staying aboard?'

'I understand they will be leaving before dinner,' he replied.

'To the showers!' Marlie ordered, grabbing an armload of decoys.

After five minutes of running up and down the companionway, bumping into each other in their hurry, not a duck was to be seen. The boxes they had packed had been set out on deck until they had hidden the others. Panting from their exertions, they hurried off the boat carrying their loads.

Marlie was of the opinion that despite his unfailing courtesy, Henry would be delighted if he never saw any of them again.

Greg will probably feel the same way, Marlie thought as she started the wagon and led her convoy through the parking lot.

If she had been able to leave two minutes earlier she would have escaped notice, but just as she turned into the main driveway of the marina lot, Greg's car turned off the public thoroughfare.

'I am not going to face him now!' Marlie muttered to herself. Mentally setting her course, and making sure of the alignment of the steering wheel, she slid down in the seat. Her last view of the sports car gave her a memorable picture of Greg's astonished face as she slid out of sight.

Marlie had calculated her course correctly, but not her slide on the seat. For a moment she lost her balance, and grabbed at the upholstered handle of the door, then back at the steering wheel. Grabbing was her mistake. She missed the wheel and clutched the horn ring. The blare from the horn was deafening. She jerked her hand away. The noise continued. She wiggled the steering wheel, throwing herself into terror of hitting something, so she raised in the seat to make sure she had not aimed the wagon into a collision course with another car.

A quick glance encompassed a group of fishermen who stared at the apparently driverless car as it crept along the driveway, blaring for attention. Behind her, Norm was frantically waving his arm, and the sports car had pulled over to the side of the road. Greg stood by the open door, wearing a puzzled, half-humorous expression.

'Drats and mice and little fishes!' Marlie muttered, wondering what to do. One thing was certain, she was not going to stop. All she needed was for Greg to walk over and offer assistance.

And he would, she thought, gritting her teeth. No matter how large that business deal was, he would not be able to resist catching her in a ridiculous position.

Raised just high enough to see between the steering wheel and the bottom of the windshield, she paused to look both ways, and pulled out on to the main road, ignoring the sign that demanded she come to a full stop.

She could feel the heat in her face as she drove at a reasonable speed up the street, inching her way up in the seat as she travelled.

Two miserable blocks later she flashed her right turn signal light and pulled over to the curb. Norm pulled in behind her, jumped from the van and came hurrying forward. He raised the hood on the wagon as she went to assist him.

Blessed quiet returned as he pulled at the horn wires.

'That's a botched up job of stopping it, but you don't want to wait two hours for a repair, do you?' He was still staring down into the engine compartment.

'Not two seconds. Let's get out of here,' Marlie snapped.

Paul came running up, followed by Sam. His grin spread all over his face.

'Boy,' he said, his voice full of admiration. 'You sure sneak out of places in style. But don't ever take up burglary—I don't think it would be your thing.'

Marlie's face, that had been fiery red because of her embarrassment, had lost some of its colour, but as her complexion darkened again, Paul backed away. Norm and Sam lost no time following him.

'Men!' Marlie stormed as she slammed the door of the wagon and turned the key. 'They're all the same!'

Some had a tendency to forget their sense of humour, too, she learned as she walked in the office of the factory after unloading the wagon.

Howard sat on the edge of his desk. The expression on his face meant trouble.

'Well, I hope you're satisfied,' he muttered.

Marlie stopped and stared. He would of course know what she had been doing. Fred would have told him. She had not asked the machine operator not to, it would have been an unfair request. But how did he know what the possible results could have been if they had not been off the yacht in time?

Had Greg called him? She wanted to ask the question, but shrank from it, fearing the answer. If Greg had called it could only have been because he was so angry he couldn't wait until after his meeting. If that were the case, what had she done to him—and what had she done to Howard?

Suddenly she saw her prank in an entirely different light. Was it just eagerness to get her own back at Greg—was that what she had been doing? She knew different. When Greg had driven away after their jealous argument, she had been afraid she would never see him again. Her entire plan had been to make sure she did. But would she? Had she been so wrapped up in herself that she had hurt Greg's business and endangered Howard's?

That little perversity that kept rearing its head, trying to force away the pain, was stirring again. She faced Howard with the determined attitude of a child who knows she deserves punishment, but hopes to avoid it.

'It was a rotten thing to do, but I didn't know he was expecting to hold a business conference there.'

'You should have expected it,' Howard snapped. 'Not everyone can spend their entire summer playing games.'

'Don't say that as if I do,' Marlie retorted, stung by his anger. Howard was usually on her side.

'I know I was wrong,' Marlie answered quietly. 'But I just thought he was out goofing off on his boat—I had no idea—' She let the words trail off. Everything she had done suddenly seemed so idiotic.

'Goofing off!' Howard snorted. 'Is that what you think I do when I come here every day?'

'I think that's a bit different,' Marlie objected. 'This is a business. That yacht is a very expensive toy. I don't know what it cost, but when someone spends that amount of money for a plaything, you have a tendency to suspect them of playing.'

Howard shook his head. 'I don't know how you could spend so much time around the man and understand nothing about him.'

Understand him? How could you love a man and not understand him? She had not believed that possible, but then she had never been in love until she met Greg Alston. She pushed that thought away. She didn't love him. She wouldn't allow herself to care about him.

'What is there to understand? He's a wealthy coupon clipper. He's rich, he's a socialite, and all he has to do is snap his fingers to have anything he wants. He leads a wasted life. I've no real use for a man like that!'

Keep saying that, the little voice said. Sooner or later you'll be convinced—maybe.

Howard snorted. 'Next, because I have a few coupons, you'll be saying I live a wasted life too.'

'You're different,' Marlie said. 'You keep something back to act as a safety bumper for the protection of the company. I know how you plan to make sure Fred, Norm and Paul will have work—if I've endangered that, I'll what I can to straighten it out.'

'I'm not worried that Greg Alston is going to take his anger at you out on me,' Howard said shortly. 'He's not that kind of man. I just think it's interesting that you think it's right for me to protect my four or five employees, yet it's a waste for him to protect his hundreds. He works a lot harder than I do, and not entirely for himself.'

'I don't see that yacht as conclusive evidence of self-sacrifice,' Marlie retorted. She was continuing an argument that was pointless, but the pain in her heart seemed to demand a struggle.

'What do you know about yachts?' Howard demanded.

'Oh, not as much as you, dear uncle, but the difference in our experience with wealth wouldn't fill a coffee cup.'

Howard leaned back, humour playing around his mouth.

'Then you recognised the boat for what it was? A fifty-year-old craft? Prime condition, of course. And he didn't spend a penny on acquisition. It's been in the family since it was new. Named after his grandmother.'

'His what?' Marlie felt as if the floor had moved.

'And you didn't pay much attention to the crew, did you? You know how attached people get to boats. How could he sell it when the crew has been serving aboard it since before he was born?'

Marlie sank in a dusty chair. The old seaman had said he had been aboard for forty-five years. She had been so busy with her prank she had paid no attention at the time.

Howard was explaining away her every objection, but

she still had one more that he couldn't answer, she thought.

'He certainly has enough time for Joan Owens-Lane,' she muttered, bringing out her last objection.

Howard laughed. 'Okay, green eyes, how would you treat the one and only daughter of a major hotel chain owner—that is, if you hoped to open exclusive shops on his premises? Most men would have paid more attention to her, and less to you, under the circumstances. It was my guess that she had hopes of making Greg part of the family. Since you've been on the scene, I don't think things have been going the way she planned.'

The telephone rang and Howard turned his attention to a sheaf of papers on the desk. Marlie strolled back to her painting table, her head lowered, her hands in the pockets of her jeans.

Had her judgment of Greg Alston been that far off? If Howard was right, she didn't know people as well as she thought.

She looked up to see Sam walking around, looking at the boxes that had been brought back from the yacht.

'I know this is the one I packed,' he was saying to Paul.

Paul was exasperated with his brother. 'What difference does it make?'

Sam rummaged in the box. He gazed at Marlie, his face showing all the misery she felt.

'It makes a lot of difference,' he muttered. 'There's a duck missing.'

'Now how could you possibly remember how many you put in there?' Norm asked with a trace of impatience. 'We were slamming them in the boxes almost too fast to count.'

Intrigued, Marlie walked over to listen.

'I didn't put it in there,' Sam argued, 'and I didn't take

it out, but I had it when I left the boat and now it's gone. It was that big one.'

'Sam,' Marlie interrupted, touched by the boy's concern, 'They were all the same size.'

'No—this one was bigger—it wasn't a carved bird, it was stuffed, I guess, with real feathers, and it was in the box when I turned around—' He went back to rummaging in the box. His worry turned to amazement as he brought out a stained and damp wrapper. 'No wooden duck did this,' he said.

'Green head?' Marlie demanded.

'Yeah,' Sam seemed surprised that she would know. 'I sat so still I thought—I didn't know it was real! I just shut the box and carried it to the van.'

'Oh, I hope he's here,' Marlie wailed. In addition to everything else, if Caesar were lost because of her joke, she'd never forgive herself.

'Caesar,' she called, looking around the boxes and under the tables. 'Someone check outside—we left the doors open—Caesar!' Marlie tried to whistle, but that was a talent she had never acquired. Paul, Norm and Sam made up for it.

Since no one else was following her orders, she left the rest to search the factory and hurried outside, around the building. She checked the street, but nothing indicated the bird had wandered in that direction. As she turned back she noticed the puddles of water that still remained in the uneven back driveway. Thinking the water might entice the duck, she walked back.

Caesar was not in any of the puddles, but just as she was completing her search, Marlie saw a pair of green legs and black and white tailfeathers, twitching with anticipation. The duck was standing very still, his long neck stretched to reach under a pile of timber. He had cornered a beetle, but couldn't quite reach it.

'Why eat bugs when you might get another hamburger?' Marlie asked him as she picked him up.

The duck made strenuous objection to being deprived of his quarry, but when Marlie sat on a low pile of wood and placed him on her lap, he found a satisfactory substitute for the bug. Sliding his bill beneath the gold band, he attempted to eat her watch.

'You're a spoiled character,' she told him, running her nails lightly through the metallic-green feathers on his head.

'You know, after they took you back to the boat, I missed you.' She sat stroking his feathers as he gave up the watch and turned to give her face an examination before deciding to pull the collar off her blouse.

'But I'll have to take you back,' she sighed. 'As much as I like you, you belong on your owner's farm. You probably shouldn't have hamburgers, and he has everything you like up there.'

'At least until his owner goes bankrupt.'

Marlie jerked around to see Greg standing behind her, his arms folded over his chest. He was wearing the same pale blue outfit he wore the day he came to the factory, only he had left the jacket behind and his long sleeves were folded back to his elbows. His dark hair and golden skin added a vividness to precise well-tailored cleanliness. Once again she was struck with the surrealistic picture he made in the shabby but respectable surroundings of the factory.

She was dressed much as she had been the first day she met him. The main difference was her hair that was being rearranged by Caesar, who had decided to remove the ribbons that held it tied above her ears. She lowered her head, staring down into the buff-and-brown feathers on Caesar's back.

'I'm sorry if I ruined your meeting,' she said. 'I had no idea you were having it, or I wouldn't have brought out the decoys. We did try to get them out of the way.'

'Yes, that helped enormously,' Greg said. 'No one would have known they were there if Trent Owens-Lane hadn't decided to check out the facilities aboard the *Veronica*. The last thing he expected was to open a shower door and be caught in a rain of wooden ducks.'

Marlie clapped her hand over her mouth to prevent a laugh. The visual picture was humorous, the probable results horrible.

'He wasn't hurt, was he?'

'Just his poise—crushed.' Greg's eyes were narrowed as he tried to keep his mouth straight. 'I'll never forgive you for taking Caesar. He should have been aboard. He'd have been the final insult to push that ass over the brink.'

Marlie's mouth formed an 'O' of surprise. Her blue eyes widened.

'You mean you didn't mind? But it must have ruined the deal you were working on—surely you're upset about that.'

Greg gave a shout of laughter. 'You can't imagine how glad I am to be out of it. I think it was worth every dime I would have made, and I include the—fringe benefit that went with. . .'

His face had hardened at his last words, and he stopped abruptly. He stepped forward and sat by her on the stack of lumber, his face and apparently his attention turned to Caesar.

Marlie knew he had said more than he thought was

proper under the circumstances. She might have mis-judged Greg in many ways, but she had learned for herself that he was a gentleman in the old-fashioned sense. He had proved that in her bedroom, though at the time she had misunderstood even that.

She had found nothing in Joan Owens-Lane to like, but still she felt pity for the woman. She was so beautiful, with social advantage and wealth behind her. Why had she found it necessary to try to buy a husband? She had not known Greg Alston either, if she thought he could be purchased as if he were some article in his chain of stores. But maybe Joan had loved him, though Marlie doubted it. If she did, Marlie was sorry for her. Greg took a large space in her own heart, too large an area to be filled by anyone else.

She kept her eyes down, not wanting him to see the schoolgirl happiness that filled her.

'I've been miserable, thinking I'd ruined things for you,' she said. She felt his arm slip around her shoulders.

'You failed this time, but I have no doubts you'll ruin me sooner or later,' he said.

Marlie looked up in surprise? How could he possibly think that? He was looking solemn and thoughtful as he met her gaze.

'I'm sure, with you around it won't be long before I'm on welfare and Caesar's in the bug line. The only man I know that can protect himself against you is Howard. I suppose the best thing for me to do is apply to him for a job when you've bankrupted me.'

He raised her chin so that she was forced to look him in the eyes. She was overcome with confusion. What was he saying? She dared not let her hopes rise, just to have them smashed again. Better to stay with the game, the thrust and jab of wit. That was what he liked. She cocked her head, giving the idea some thought while she retied one of the ribbons that Caesar had pulled free.

'Quite possibly Howard would give you a job,' she murmured as if she were giving the matter serious consideration. 'You do know how to run the Howler. That reminds me of a question. Why did you want to run the machine? You said you would tell us after you worked out your idea.'

'I'll never tell,' he said, his chin thrust forward with playful hauteur.

Marlie lowered her brows in a mock frown. 'Just as I thought! You came to steal our industrial secrets.'

'Of course,' he sounded surprised. 'Didn't you know that was my main occupation? By tomorrow the entire world will know your mallards have green heads.'

Marlie laughed at his remark, her heart filled with love and happiness simply because he was with her. At the moment she felt life could hold no more happiness.

'Seriously, what was your idea? Perhaps Howard and Fred could lay it out for you.'

'I don't need their help.'

His answer had been so short it shocked Marlie. She wondered if she had stumbled on sensitive feelings. The flicker in his eyes, and a change of expression told her he had noticed. He put his arm around her, his hand on her shoulder.

'It's too late, you see. After my trip to Norway, I had a terrific idea. Bureau valets in the shape of viking longboats. Totally new concept.'

Marlie's frown was genuine. Which would be best, she wondered. Should she flatter his ego or tell him the truth? The idea was far from original. She decided the truth would be best. Even if he were disappointed, that would be better than letting him bring out a well-used idea as his own. That could be embarrassing later.

'It's a good idea, but there have been some on the market,' she said slowly. 'In fact, I gave my father one two years ago.'

'And probably bought it in Alston's,' he said, laughing. 'The next how-to book on spying should include a chapter on not stealing from yourself. When I saw one in my own store, I felt like a fool.'

Her heart skipped a beat as she saw that engaging, almost childlike smile appear again. At that moment he resembled a little boy, caught in a foolish prank. She wanted to put her arms around him, reassuring him his next idea would be the greatest ever, but she was committed to the game. She shrugged.

'Then I don't know how Howard could hire you. You're obviously not original in your thinking. Your only talent seems to be making millions. We make ducks.'

'I see what you mean,' Greg appeared thoughtful. 'Do you think I'd have a better chance with him if I married into the family?'

Married? Into the family? Marlie's gaze flew to his. There was no mistaking the laughter, mixed with tenderness. Her lips parted to answer but at that moment her view of Greg was blocked as Caesar stood up, putting his head between theirs.

'You and your ducks!' Greg growled in impatience. He pushed Caesar off Marlie's lap, sending the bird off in his lopsided flight. Caesar gave an angry quack and went back in search of the beetle. As he waddled along, his green legs and feet were brightened by the summer sun.

'Mine?' Marlie cried. 'Caesar is your duck!'

'And that's another thing,' Greg eyed her sternly. 'I know you have this problem with paint, but when I feel like an explanation, I want to know why my ducks have green feet.'

Marlie opened her mouth to tell him, but she was interrupted by his lips on hers. As her arms encircled him, she decided she could make her explanations later. Then she'd kick him.